'*You're* coming to work here?'

'That's right,' Cam told her in his gentlest, most encouraging tone. The one he usually used to calm barking dogs and tearful small children. 'I'm the new doctor.' He offered another smile. 'Not exactly looking the part at the moment, I'll admit, but I polish up okay.'

'You can't be the new doctor,' Jo continued. 'I asked for a mature woman with a motherly manner—not for some overgrown adolescent male with a painted van and three surfboards and probably the counselling skills of an aardvark.'

Cam bit back an urge to ask if aardvarks had *any* counselling skills, and if so how she knew. This wasn't the moment to make light of the situation.

'Maybe I was all they had?' he suggested.

NEW DOC
IN TOWN

BY
MEREDITH WEBBER

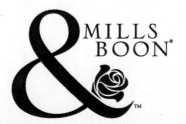

First published in Great Britain 2011
by Mills & Boon, an imprint of Harlequin (UK) Limited.
Large Print edition 2012
Harlequin (UK) Limited, Eton House,
18-24 Paradise Road, Richmond, Surrey TW9 1SR

© Meredith Webber 2011

ISBN: 978 0 263 22452 8

Harlequin (UK) policy is to use papers that are
natural, renewable and recyclable products and made
from wood grown in sustainable forests. The logging
and manufacturing process conform to the legal
environmental regulations of the country of origin.

Printed and bound in Great Britain
by CPI Antony Rowe, Chippenham, Wiltshire

Meredith Webber says of herself, 'Once, I read an article which suggested that Mills and Boon was looking for new Medical™ Romance authors. I had one of those "I can do that" moments, and gave it a try. What began as a challenge has become an obsession—though I do temper the "butt on seat" career of writing with dirty but healthy outdoor pursuits, fossicking through the Australian Outback in search of gold or opals. Having had some success in all of these endeavours, I now consider I've found the perfect lifestyle.'

Recent titles by the same author:

MELTING THE ARGENTINE DOCTOR'S HEART
TAMING DR TEMPEST
SHEIKH, CHILDREN'S DOCTOR...HUSBAND

These books are also available in ebook format from www.millsandboon.co.uk

CHAPTER ONE

THE psychedelic camper-van spun through the entry to the parking lot with a squeal of tyres, startling Jo as she inserted the key into the dead-lock on the surgery door. She watched, fingers tightening on the key she'd just turned, as a man in tattered board shorts and a bright Hawaiian-print shirt emerged from the van.

A very tall man, thickset.

With very broad shoulders.

Her heart might have skipped a beat but that didn't stop her medical mind checking the man out.

He didn't seem to be bleeding, and he wasn't limping or doubled over in pain, so sending him on to the hospital was definitely the best idea…

Definitely!

But do it politely.

Don't freak him out.

Calm voice, no sudden moves.

'I'm sorry but the clinic is closed,' she called out to him. Took a deep breath and added, 'If you follow the main road down through two round-abouts then turn right at the third you'll find the hospital. It has twenty-four-hour Accident and Emergency cover.'

Jo—Dr Joanna Harris to give her full title—carefully unlocked the door she'd just locked, and prayed that she sounded confident. The man didn't move, standing motionless beside the van, studying her with a slight frown on his face, as if her words hadn't made sense.

Then, like the sun bursting through clouds on a showery day, the frown cleared and the big man smiled.

Against all common sense Jo felt her tension ease, which was ridiculous given that the local pharmacy had been robbed three times in the last six months.

'Shouldn't there be more than one person lock-ing up a medical clinic?' the giant asked, his deep voice rumbling up from somewhere inside a broad chest that was barely hidden by the hula girls, hibiscus flowers and palm trees—a lot of palm trees.

Tension returned despite the fact the voice

was warm—teasing almost—and held no hint of threat.

'There are no drugs kept on the premises,' Jo told him, pointing to a large sign posted on the glass door.

'Do people actually believe those signs?' the stranger asked, and though she knew people probably didn't, Jo defended her sign.

'Of course they do! *And* we've got cameras.' She pointed to the camera angled downward from the corner of the building. 'Now, if you'd just move your vehicle, I can put up the chain across the car-park entrance. We're not open at all on Sunday. I was doing some tidying up.'

Stupid thing to say—now he'd *know* there was no one else around—although he'd probably guessed that when he'd seen her locking up. Maybe it was because the man wasn't sending out scary vibes that she'd been prattling on to him.

She still had her fingers on the key and the key was in the lock and she was pretty sure she could get inside before he reached her if he *did* make a move in her direction.

Cam studied the woman who was resolutely—and foolishly—guarding the clinic entrance. She was a midget—five-three at the most, slim built but curvy for all that, and with a wild tangle of pale red hair—yet she was standing her ground.

He'd driven in on a whim, noticing the sign— Crystal Cove Medical Clinic—at the last minute, wanting to see the place, not expecting anyone to be there on a Sunday morning. It hadn't been until he was out of the van that he'd seen the woman. Now he was trying to look as non-threatening as possible, arms hanging loosely at his sides, joints relaxed, although there was no way he could minimise his six-three height.

'I'll be going,' he said, keeping his voice as soft and low as he could. 'I noticed the sign as I was driving past and thought I'd take a look. I'm coming to work here, you see.'

Even across the car park he saw the woman turn so pale he thought she might faint, while her loss of colour made a wash of faint golden freckles stand out on her skin.

'You're coming to *work* here?' she demanded. '*You're* coming to work here?'

'That's right,' Cam told her in his gentlest, most encouraging tone. The one he usually used to calm barking dogs and tearful small children.

And women who maybe weren't the sharpest knife in the drawer. This one had had to repeat his words a couple of times before she got the picture.

'I'm the new doctor,' he added. After all, people were usually reassured by doctors. 'Got the job through Personal Medical Recruitments in Sydney.' He offered another smile. 'Not exactly looking the part at the moment, I'll admit, but I polish up okay.'

'You can't be the new doctor,' the woman wailed, and shook her head so bits of hair flew everywhere. 'You can't *possibly* be! You're a *man*!'

Well, he could hardly deny the man part, but he was definitely a doctor, so Cam waited for more.

It wasn't long in coming.

'I asked for a mature woman,' she continued, 'preferably over forty, with counselling experience and a motherly manner, not for some overgrown adolescent male with a painted van and three surfboards and probably the counselling skills of an aardvark.'

Cam bit back an urge to ask if aardvarks had any counselling skills and if so how she knew. This wasn't the moment to make light of the situation.

'Maybe I was all they had,' he suggested, although he was well aware he'd conned the woman at the medical recruitment agency into offering him this particular job, using every bit of charm he could dredge up because the surf at Crystal Cove was reputed to be some of the best on the east coast. Geographically, the spot was a perfect stopping-off place on his planned surfing safari. A high, rocky headland reached out into the sea, so if the southerlies were blowing the sheltered north cove would have good surf, while leaving effective swells on the open beach a few days later.

He'd thought he could fill in a few months here quite happily, working and surfing. The working part was important, as he knew there'd be times he couldn't surf—flat sea, bad weather. He didn't want to have long days doing nothing because doing nothing left him too much time for thinking, too much time for remembering the horrors he'd seen. 'And I've not only done extra courses on counselling, but I'm good at it.'

His gut twisted as he said it, and it took all his skill at closing the many doors in his mind to shut away memories of the kind of counselling he'd done. He smiled to cover the momentary lapse.

Jo finally turned to face the man she'd been talking to over her shoulder, although she left the key in the lock. Living in a community where just about everyone rode the waves on one kind of board or another, she was used to seeing men with their over-long hair turned to, mostly temporary, dreadlocks by the salt, so this man's brown, matted, sun-streaked hair wasn't *so* unusual. Neither was his tanned face, which made his pale eyes—he was too far away to see a colour—seem paler, and his teeth, now he smiled, seem whiter.

The smile was good, but he was probably the kind of man who knew that—knew the power of a charming smile.

Charming?

Was it *that* good?

She'd certainly relaxed!

Annoyed by this self-revelation, she stiffened her resolve.

'I'm sorry but I really don't think it will work out. I didn't ask for a woman on a whim, or because I can't work with men—in fact, the former owner of the practice was a man and I worked with him for years. It's just that...'

She couldn't *begin* to list all the reasons this man would be an impossible employee.

'Just that?' he prompted, smiling again but helpfully this time.

'Just that it's impossible!' Jo snapped, but even as she said it, she realised how stupid this was, to be having the conversation across half the parking lot—the man standing where he'd emerged from the van, she on the surgery steps. 'Oh, come up to the house,' she added crossly, then shook her head. 'No, show me some authorisation and identification first—something from the agency, your driver's licence, anything.'

He reached back into the van and brought out a quite respectable-looking briefcase, tan leather, a bit battered, but in not bad condition. He opened it and withdrew a file.

'It's all in here,' he said, walking towards her.

He walked well, very upright, yet with an unconscious grace. She could picture him on a surfboard, cutting across the face of a wave, a conqueror of the ocean, sun glinting off the water droplets on that chest...

Jo gave herself a mental head-slap—a reminder to stay with it, although the longing that had come with the thought of riding the sea remained like a bruise in her chest. The man was still a stranger for all he knew the name of the agency she used to recruit staff, *and* held himself in an unthreatening manner. Reading body language was something she'd had to learn, but he, too, could have learned it.

He stopped a reasonable distance from her and passed her the file, then stepped back. Yep, he'd done the same body language course! Maybe he was the genuine article. but she'd wanted a woman.

She opened the file and stared at the photo it contained. Surely the gorgeous male with the short back and sides hairstyle, the dark arched eyebrows over pale blue-grey eyes, the long straight nose and shapely lips quirked, in the photo, into a slight smile wasn't the surfie type standing right in front of her.

She looked from the photo to the man and saw the eyes, blue-grey, and then the same quirky, half-embarrassed smile, although the beard stubble she could see now he was closer to her hid the shapely lips.

'Fraser Cameron?'

A quick, decisive nod.

'I'm usually called Cam. I'd just got out of the army when they took the photo,' the man explained. 'I had an interview with the agency, put in my résumé, promised to keep in touch by phone and went surfing for a while. Nothing like a few years in the desert to give you a longing for the ocean. Deserts and ocean—well, they have sand in common but that's about all.'

As job interviews went, this wasn't going too well. Cam had realised that from the start. It was becoming increasingly obvious that the young woman in front of him was his boss-to-be, and she didn't seem too happy about any aspect of him, even apart from the fact he wasn't female.

Not that he could blame her. He should have had a shower at the beach and washed the salt out of his hair—at least run a comb through it. But until he'd seen the sign for the surgery and driven in on a whim, he'd been intent on finding a caravan park and having a proper hot shower and shave for the first time in, what—four days? He rubbed his hand across his chin—no, maybe only three. He'd stopped in Port Macquarie and had a shave there…

She was reading through his résumé, glancing up at him from time to time as if trying to fit the printed words to the unshaven man in front of her, and the fact that she was occupied gave Cam the chance to study her in turn.

The wild hair was probably the bane of her life, untamed curls that would refuse to do what she required of them. Today she'd tugged her hair into some kind of clip thing on the top of her head but, like Medusa's snakes, strands were curling out from the containment and glinting a vibrant red-gold in the sun. Her skin went with the red hair—pale and freckled, almost milk white at her temples and so fine he could see the blue line of a blood vessel beneath it. Would he feel the throb of her heartbeat if he kissed that blue thread?

The thought startled him so much he took a step backwards, just as she looked up, clear green eyes fixed on him—still shooting darts of suspicion in his direction.

'I guess you are who you say you are,' she muttered, so obviously put out at having to make the admission he had to smile.

'But still not a woman,' he reminded her, the temptation to tease her too strong to resist.

She shot him a glare that might have affected a lesser man, but he'd grown up with three sisters, all of whom were good glarers, so he met it with a smile, although he knew—also thanks to his siblings—it would make her angrier.

'The house is this way,' she said, leading him across the front of the clinic building then along the side of it to where steep steps climbed towards a house that must look north over the ocean. From the bottom of the steps he could see how the clever architect had cantilevered the building out from the steep slope, and he could imagine the magnificent view of the ocean whoever lived in the house must enjoy.

'Wow!'

He could say no more for the stairway ended on the wide deck of the house he'd admired from below, and the sweep of beach and ocean, the high headland protecting the corner of the bay, and more ocean beyond it simply took his breath away.

'You would have seen the whales migrating north at the beginning of winter, but they're heading south now with their calves, on their long journey home to Antarctica.'

He glanced at the woman who'd offered this titbit of information. She was standing not far away, and he knew from the expression on her face that no matter how often she looked out at this unbelievably beautiful view it would never pall for her. Just seeing it had softened her mood enough for her to share her joy in the annual whale migration.

Softened it enough to accept him as an employee?

'I gather you are Dr Harris?' he said, wishing he'd asked more about his prospective employer when the woman from the agency had discussed the job. In truth, from the moment she'd mentioned Crystal Cove, he'd been so busy convincing her he would be perfect for the job he'd barely asked a question.

She was smiling now, the petite redhead on the deck with him, smiling and shaking her head.

'Ask that question of anyone in town and they'll say no. Dr Harris was my father, but I am a doctor, Joanna Harris, Dr Jo, or just plain Jo to the locals, most of whom have known me all my life. Some of the older ones are still, though I've been back for five years, a bit dubious about trusting me to diagnose their problems or prescribe medication for their ills. It's because they did that dandling me on their knee thing years ago and can't believe I've grown up.'

'You took over your father's practice?' It was stupid to be asking the obvious but there'd been tension in Joanna Harris's voice and he wondered if it was simply to do with the locals not accepting her entirely, or to do with something else.

'His practice, his house, his life,' she responded, sounding happier now, even smiling. 'My mother died when I was young and Dad brought me and my sister up, then, whammo, two years ago he met a woman who sailed in here on a yacht, and he fell in love. His life is now with her, wandering the world, it's wonderful!'

Faint colour in her cheeks and a shine in her eyes told Cam she was genuinely happy for her father, so why the tension earlier?

And did it matter?

He was coming to work for this woman, he didn't need to know what made her tick.

'But taking over his practice? Was that not so wonderful?'

Okay, so what made people tick fascinated him—he'd *had* to ask!

Jo studied the man who'd erupted into her life. So she'd told him about her dad going off, but did that give him the right to pry further into her life? And why ask that particular question? What had she said to make him think her life back in Crystal Cove was anything but perfect?

It wasn't, of course, and probably never would be, not entirely, and especially not if the refuge closed because without the refuge she'd have time on her hands—time to think—and that meant letting all the mess of grief and guilt from Jilly's death come flooding back. That definitely wasn't his business.

She had no intention of answering his questions, now or ever. Neither was he staying. With school holidays looming and the town due to double or even triple in population for a couple of months, maybe he'd have to stay until the agency found her someone more suitable, but permanently?

No way!

The problem was, given that he was on her front deck, what did she do with him right now? She had to say *something*.

Politeness dictated the answer.

'Would you like a coffee, tea, a cold drink?'

She looked up at him as she asked the question and saw the white lines fanning out from his eyes where he'd smiled, or squinted, in the sun. She saw lines of stress in his face as well. A photo taken when he'd just left the army? An army doctor? In this day and age most army doctors would have been deployed in war zones overseas. He'd mentioned deserts. Of course there'd be lines of stress in his face.

'Water is fine,' he replied, and she guessed he was probably as uncomfortable as she was.

'I'm making coffee,' she persisted, 'so it's no trouble.'

He looked down at her, a slight frown on his face.

'Water's fine,' he repeated, then he crossed to the edge of the deck and looked out over the ocean.

Jo hurried into the house, anxious to read more of the file she held in her hands. It was strange that the agency hadn't contacted her to let her know the man was coming—although maybe it was because he *was* a man they'd neglected to contact her. They *knew* she wanted a woman; they even knew why.

The kitchen faced the deck so she could keep an eye on the stranger as she popped a capsule into her coffee machine. While the milk heated, she flicked through the pages, coming to a highlighted passage about Dr Fraser Cameron's second degree in psychology and his counselling experience. Had the agency highlighted it, or had they told him what she wanted so he'd highlighted it himself?

He'd been counselling young soldiers in a war zone? Doing more than counselling, too, no doubt.

Putting young men and women back together physically as well as mentally.

The very thought made Jo's stomach tighten.

But hard as his job must have been, how would it relate to counselling women in a refuge?

The refuge…

If it closed it wouldn't matter one jot whether the man could counsel women or not.

If it closed she wouldn't need another doctor in the practice…

Jo sighed then stiffened, straightening her shoulders and reinforcing her inner determination.

The refuge was *not* going to close!

What's more, if this man was going to stay, even in the short term, he'd have to help her make sure it didn't.

She poured the milk into her coffee, filled a glass with water from the refrigerator, and headed back to the deck.

'Did the agency explain the type of counselling you'd be required to do?' she asked him as he came towards the table where she'd set down their drinks.

The little frown she'd noticed earlier deepened and he shook his head, then shrugged shoulders that were so broad she wondered how he fitted through a doorway.

Shoulders?

Why was she thinking of shoulders? Worse, when had she last even noticed physical attributes in a man, yet here she was seeing lines in his face, and checking on shoulders…

'They said you wanted someone with counselling experience because although there was a psychologist in Crystal Cove, he, or maybe it was a she, was already overworked. I assumed you probably ran well-men and well-women clinics, sex education at the schools and parenting skills courses. You'd be likely to use counselling as part of these.'

Jo sighed.

'The women's refuge wasn't mentioned?'

His reaction was a blank stare, followed by a disbelieving 'Women's refuge? The town has a population of what, thirty-five hundred and you have a women's refuge?'

'The area has a much larger population—small farms, villages, acreage lots where people have retired or simply moved in. Anyway, just because women live in a small town, does that mean they're not entitled to a safe place to go?'

Had she snapped that he held up his hands in surrender?

'Hey,' he said. 'I'm sorry! No way I meant that, but it came as a shock, the refuge thing. No wonder you took one look at me and saw me as a disaster. My size alone is enough to frighten horses, not to mention vulnerable women, but surely we can work through this. Surely the women who use the refuge come in contact with other men in their lives, men who aren't threatening to them? And wouldn't it be a good thing if they did? If they got to know men who *didn't* threaten them? Men who are just as horrified by what is happening to them, and just as empathetic with them, as a woman counsellor would be?'

He was right, of course! One of the refuge's strongest supporters was Mike Sinclair, the officer in charge of the local police force, while Tom Fletcher, head of the small local hospital, was loved by all the women who used the refuge. But the refuge aside, did she want this man working for her?

The answer that sprang immediately to mind was a firm no, but when she questioned it she

didn't like the reasons. They were far too personal. She was judging the man on his appear-
ance, not his ability—judging him on the effect
he was having on *her*.

Anyway, did she have a choice but to accept
him?

Not right now.

'I suppose you'll have to do,' she said, hoping it
hadn't come out as an unwilling mutter. 'But it's a
trial, you have to understand that. I'm not promising it will work out, but right now I'm desperate. The town doubles in size in school holidays,
which begin officially in a fortnight, but before
that we have the wonderful invasion of schoolies.'

'Schoolies? You have schoolies coming here?'

And although she dreaded the annual influx of
school-leavers every year, Jo still felt affronted
that the man would think her town not good
enough for them.

'Not all school leavers want the bright lights of
Surfers' Paradise,' she said defensively.

'Ha!' he said, blue eyes twinkling at her in a
most disconcerting manner. 'Bet you wish they
hadn't discovered Crystal Cove!'

She considered denying his assumption, but
knew she couldn't. He'd be working with her so

he could hardly avoid seeing how frazzled she became as she worried about drunk, sick and sometimes very unhappy teenagers who were supposedly marking some rite of passage into adulthood.

Adulthood? They had as much sense as fleas, some of them…

'You're right. It's only in recent years that young people have decided the Cove is cool enough for them. Most of those who come are keen surfers and they're not a problem. Anyway, I'll take you on but, as I said, we'll have to see how things work out.'

'I don't mind that,' the stranger—Cam—said calmly. 'After all, I might not like working with you either, and there's still a lot of coastline for me to cover in my surfing odyssey.'

She was about to take affront—again!—but realised he was right.

'Fair call,' she told him, ignoring the smirk that had accompanied his words. 'Now, once the schoolies arrive—that's next week—there'll be no time to show you around so—'

She didn't want to sound desperate but, given the situation at the refuge and the fact that she needed some free time to try to sort out funding problems there, she actually *was* desperate.

'Can you start tomorrow? No, that's stupid. Can you start now so I can show you the clinic, introduce you at the hospital, and give you a quick tour of the town?'

Was she looking dubious that he glanced down at his attire and raised his eyebrows at her, the amused expression on his face sparking an unexpected—and totally inappropriate—flicker of warmth deep inside her body?

This *definitely* wasn't a good idea!

'Like this?' he said, then shook his head. 'Give me an hour to check in at the caravan park and have a shower and shave. I wouldn't want to give people the wrong first impression.'

The man's amused expression turned into a smile—her stupid flicker graduated to a flutter in her chest that caused another mental head slap.

Reality added a harder slap, this one bringing her down to earth with such a thud her physical reactions to the man paled into insignificance.

'It's no good. You won't find a patch of grass available at the caravan park,' she told him, gloom shadowing the words. 'Well, there might be something for the next few days but after that you'd be out on your ear. Most of the schoolies camp there, then during the school holidays regulars book the same sites from year to year. It's a similar situation with the flats and units in town. Most of them are holiday rentals and, although you wouldn't be looking for something permanent because we don't know if it will work out, there'd be nothing available right now.'

Not put off by the despair in her voice, he was still grinning when he suggested, 'Is there a shower in your medical centre? Will the council evict me or fine you if I camp in the parking area?'

Jo rolled her eyes.

'Great—here comes Dr Cameron, emerging from his van in the parking area. I can just imagine what people would think!' The words came out snappish but she knew she was more annoyed with the offer she'd have to make than with the man himself.

She told herself not to be feeble, straightened her shoulders, and made the offer.

'There's a flat.'

'You make it sound like the castle of doom!' Cam teased, wondering why the woman was looking so unhappy about the revelation. Although she'd hardly been joyous about anything since his arrival. 'Rats? Spiders? Snakes? Cockroaches big as dogs?'

'It's here at the house,' she muttered, sounding even more unhappy, although now he could understand why she was wary. It would be awkward to have a strange man living so close, though if she'd checked out his credentials and read through his references, she shouldn't be too worried. 'Out the back. Dad built it years ago and I used it for a while until he took off on the yacht. It's got a deck, the flat not the yacht, although—'

She stopped, probably aware she was dithering, and she drew a deep, calming breath.

'The deck on the flat—it's not as big as this, but it has the northerly view. In the past, since Dad left, I've hired locums at holiday times and they've used it.'

Temporarily.

She didn't say the word but Cam heard it in her voice. He could understand her reluctance to have a fellow-worker living in such close proximity full time but if locums had done so up till now…

Maybe she had a set against men?

Been hurt by one?

Realising he should be thinking about the job,

not the woman who was hiring him, he turned his attention back to the subject.

'I understood that although there'd be a trial period, you were looking for someone for a permanent position this time, not a locum. Has the town grown? Do you want to cut down on your own workload?'

She studied him for a moment, as if debating whether he was worth answering, then gave a deep sigh.

'The town's grown, a second practice opened but no sooner did that happen than the hospital had staff cuts, then the second practice closed, and with the refuge—well, I decided it was time to expand.'

The explanation rattled from her lips—nice lips, very pale pink, distracting him again—and Cam understood enough to know that the flat, like the job, was only temporary. While she might have been happy having a fortyish woman living permanently in close proximity to her, having a large male surfer was a different story.

'I'll show you over it then you'll have to go back down the steps to the car park and drive along the road towards the highway, taking the first left to bring you up the hill and around to the carport.'

All business now, she led him off the deck, through a sparsely furnished living area. It was functional and uncluttered, decorated in sand colours, but with wide windows giving views of the sea in all directions, the room didn't need decoration.

It was like the woman herself, functional and uncluttered, he decided, following a decidedly shapely bottom in khaki cargo shorts, a khaki singlet top completing her outfit.

A decidedly shapely bottom?

Well, he couldn't help but notice, any more than he could have helped noticing the pink lips earlier. Was noticing such things about his boss unprofessional behaviour?

So many years in the army had left him unprepared for the niceties of civilian life, particularly where women were concerned. He held a mental conversation with his sisters and came to the conclusion that while thinking his boss had a shapely butt was okay, mentioning his opinion of it or of any other part of her anatomy, to her or anyone else, would definitely be unwise.

CHAPTER TWO

A BREEZEWAY divided the house from the little building perched beside it on the steep hillside.

'A double carport so you can keep your van under cover,' his guide said, waving her left hand to indicate the covered parking spaces. She reached above the door for a key, saying, 'I know I shouldn't keep it there,' before inserting it in the lock and opening the door.

The flat was as different from the minimalist-style house as it was possible to be. Roses, not giant cockroaches! The roses dominated the small space. They bloomed from trellises on the wallpaper, glowed on the fabric covering the small lounge suite, while silk ones stood in vases on small tables here and there.

'Ha!' Cam said, unable to stop himself. 'You wanted a fortyish woman to fit in with the furnishings, although…'

He turned towards his new boss and caught a

look of such sadness on her face he wished he
hadn't opened his mouth. Though now he had,
he had to finish what he'd been about to say or
look even more foolish than he felt.

'Well, one of my sisters is forty and roses definitely aren't her thing.'

The words came out strained, mumbled almost
under his breath, but he doubted Joanna Harris
heard them. She'd moved across the small room
and opened the sliding glass windows, walking
out through them onto the deck.

The way she stood, hugging herself at the railing, told him she wanted—perhaps needed—to
be alone, so he explored the neatly organised
domain, finding two small bedrooms, a bathroom
and a kitchen had been fitted somehow into the
tiny flat. The configuration of the bathroom made
him wonder. There was a shower above a tiled
floor, no cubicle, just a floor waste where most
of the water would go. The basin was set low, no
cupboard beneath it.

This and a silver bar screwed onto the wall at
waist height suggested the room had been built
for someone with a disability and now he looked
around he realised the doorways were wider than

normal—to accommodate a wheelchair?—and hand-grips had been installed in other places.

Jo had spoken of a sister...

A disabled sister?

He looked out at the figure standing on the deck, a hundred questions flashing through his mind, but the way she stood—the way she'd handled his arrival and their conversation since—told him he might never have those questions answered.

A very private person, Jo Harris, or so he suspected, although on an hour's acquaintance how could he be judging her?

She should have redecorated the flat, Jo chided herself. She should have done it as soon as she'd moved into it after Jilly died—yet she'd always felt that changing the roses her sister had loved would have been letting go of her twin for ever.

A betrayal of some kind.

And surely 'should' was the unkindest word in the English language, so filled with regrets of what might have been, or not been. Should have done this, should not have done that. Her own list of shoulds could go on for ever, should have come home from Sydney sooner being right at the top of it!

Jo hugged her body and looked out to sea, waiting for the view to calm her, for her mind to shut away the memories and consign the shoulds to the trash bin she kept tucked away in her head. Coming into the flat usually upset her—not a lot—just brought back memories, but today, seeing the stranger—Cam—there, he'd looked so out of place among the roses Jill had loved, it had hurt more than usual.

'I'll bring my car up.'

He called to her from the doorway and before she could turn he was gone. Good! It would give her time to collect herself. Actually, it would give her time to scurry back to her place and hide from the man for the rest of the day, though that was hardly fair.

She found a little notebook on the kitchen bench and scribbled a note. 'Will meet you in the carport in half an hour, we can get a bite to eat in town and I'll show you around.'

A bite to eat in town.

It sounded so innocuous but within an hour of being seen down the street with him the word would be all over town that Jo Harris had finally found a man!

As if a man who looked like him—like the picture of him anyway—would be interested in a scrawny redhead.

Of course once the locals realised he'd come to work for her, the talk would settle down, then when he left...

She shook her head, unable to believe she'd been thinking that maybe it would be nice to have a man around.

A man or *this* man?

She had a sneaky suspicion the second option was the answer but she wouldn't consider it now. Instant attraction was something for books, not real people—not real people like her, anyway.

The man would be her colleague—temporary colleague—and right now she had to show him around the town. She'd re-clip her hair and smear on a little lightly coloured sunscreen, the only make-up she ever used, but she wouldn't change—no need to really startle the town by appearing in anything other than her usual garb.

Unfortunately as she passed through the kitchen she saw his résumé, still open on the bench—open at the photo...

She added lipstick to the preparations. After all, it, too, had sun protection.

Leaving the house, she drove down to the clinic

first, showing him around the consulting and treatment rooms, proud of the set-up and pleased when he praised it. Then back in the car, she took Cam to the top of the rise so he could see the town spread out below them.

'It's fairly easy to get around,' she explained to him. 'As you can see from here, the cove beach faces north and the southern beach—the long one—faces east.'

'With the shopping centre running along the esplanade behind the cove, is that right?'

He pointed to the wide drive along the bay side, Christmas decorations already flapping in the wind.

'There's actually a larger, modern shopping mall down behind this hill,' Jo told him. 'You just drive up here and turn right instead of left. We're going the other way because the best cafés are on the front and the hospital is also down there. Until the surfing craze started, the cove beach was the one everyone used. It's only been in relatively recent years that the open beach has become popular and land along it has been developed for housing.'

Explaining too much?

Telling him stuff he didn't need to know?

Yes to both but Jo felt so uncomfortable with the stranger in her car, she knew the silence would prickle her skin if she didn't fill it with talk.

'Can we eat before we visit the hospital?' her passenger asked, and although there was nothing in his voice to give him away, memories of her own surfing days came rushing back to Jo. When the surf was running, food had been the last thing on her mind, so she'd return home close to lunchtime, *starving*.

'Don't tell me you haven't had breakfast?' she wailed. 'I realised you'd come straight from the beach but...'

She turned so she could see his face.

'You should have said,' she told him, mortified that she'd been proudly pointing out up-to-date equipment while all he wanted was something to eat. 'I could have offered you food at the house—cereal or toast or something. It was just so late in the morning I didn't think of it. Or we could have gone straight to the café instead of doing the clinic tour first.'

She'd turned her attention back to the road but heard the smile in his voice when he replied.

'Hey, don't go beating yourself up about it. I'm a big boy. I can look after myself.'

'Hardly a boy!' Jo snapped, contrarily angry now, although it wasn't her fault the man was starving.

She pulled up opposite her favourite café, a place she and Jill had hung out in during their early high-school days.

'They do an all-day big breakfast I can recommend,' she told Cam, before dropping down out of the car and crossing the road, assuming he would follow. As she heard his door shut, she used the remote lock and heard the ping as the car was secured.

'A big breakfast will hit the spot,' Cam declared as he studied the blackboard menu and realised that the combination of eggs, bacon, sausages, tomato, beans and toast was just what he needed to fill the aching void in his stomach.

If only other voids in other parts of him could be filled as easily...

'I'll have a toasted cheese and—'

'Tomato sandwich and a latte,' the young girl who'd come to take their orders finished.

'One day I'll order something different,' Jo warned her, and the girl laughed as she turned to Cam.

'The sky will turn green the day Jo changes her order,' she said. 'And for you?'

He ordered the big breakfast, absolutely famished now he'd started thinking about food and how long it had been since he'd eaten. He looked out across the road at the people gathered on the beach, and beyond them to where maybe a dozen surfers sat on their boards, waiting for a wave that might never come.

He understood their patience. It wasn't for the waves that he surfed, or not entirely. He surfed to clear his head—to help to banish the sights and sounds of war that disturbed his nights and haunted his days.

He surfed to heal himself, or so he hoped.

'The surf was far better this morning,' he said, turning his mind from things he couldn't control and his attention back to his companion.

'Higher tide and an offshore breeze. Now the wind's stronger from the west and flattening the surf but those kids will sit out there anyway. They don't mind if there are no waves, and now they're all pretty good about wearing sun protection it's a healthy lifestyle for them.'

She spoke in a detached manner, as if her mind was on something else. Intriguing, that's what his new boss was, especially as she'd been frowning as she'd explained surf conditions in Crystal Bay—surely not bothersome information.

'So why the frown?' Yes, he *was* intrigued.

'What frown?'

'You've been frowning since the girl took our order,' he pointed out.

A half-embarrassed smile slid across his new boss's lips, which she twisted slightly before answering.

'If you must know, I was thinking how predictable I've become, or maybe how boring I am that I don't bother thinking of something different to have for lunch. This place does great salads, but do I order a roast pumpkin, feta and pine-nut concoction? No, just boring old toasted cheese and tomato. I've got to get a life!'

Cam chuckled at the despair in her voice.

'I wouldn't think ordering the same thing for lunch every day prohibits you from having a life.'

Fire flashed in her eyes again and he found himself enjoying the fact that he could stir her, not necessarily stir her to anger, but at least fire some spark in the woman who was…different in some way?

No, intriguing was the only word.

'Of course it doesn't, and if my life wasn't so full I wouldn't need to employ another doctor, but the cheese and tomato is a symbol, that's all.'

Small-scale glare—about a four.

'A symbol? Cheese and tomato—toasted—a symbol?'

Now the eyes darkened, narrowed.

'You know very well what I mean. It's not the cheese and tomato, it's the repetition thing. We get stuck in a groove—well, not you obviously or you wouldn't be wandering along the coast in a psychedelic van, but me, I'm stuck in a groove.'

'With a cheese and tomato sandwich, most un-comfortable,' he teased, and saw the anger flare before she cooled it with a reluctant grimace and a head shake.

'It's all very well for you to mock,' she told him sternly. 'You've been off seeing the world with the army. You don't know what it's like to be stuck in a small town.'

She hesitated, frowning again, before adding, 'That came out sounding as if I resented being here, which I don't. I love the Cove, love living here, love working here—so stuck is the wrong word. It's just that I think maybe people in small towns are more likely to slip into grooves than people in big cities.'

He had to laugh.

'Lady, you don't know nothin' about grooves until you've been in the army. *Everyone* in the army has a groove. It's the only way a thing that big can work. Hence the psychedelic van you mentioned—that's my way of getting out of my particular groove.'

And away from the memories...

Jo studied the man who'd made the joking remark and saw the truth behind it in the bruised shadows under his eyes and the lines that strain, not age, had drawn on his cheeks. She had an uncomfortable urge to touch him, to rest her hand on his arm where it lay on the table, just for a moment, a touch to say she understood his need to escape so much reality.

He's not staying!

The reminder echoed around inside her head and she kept her hands to herself, smiling as their meals arrived and she saw Cam's eyes widening when he realised how big a big breakfast was in Crystal Cove.

'Take your time,' she told him, 'I could sit here and look out at the people on the beach all day.'

Which was true enough, but although she watched the people on the beach, her mind was churning with other things.

Common sense dictated that if she was employing another doctor for the practice it should be a man. A lot of her male patients would prefer to see a man, especially about personal problems they might be having. Elderly men in particular were reluctant to discuss some aspects of their health, not so much with a woman but with a woman they'd known since she was a child.

She'd ignored common sense and asked for a woman for a variety of reasons, most to do with the refuge. Not that her practice and the refuge were inextricably entwined, although as the only private practice in town she was called in whenever a woman or child at the refuge needed a doctor.

Mind you, with a man—she cast a sidelong glance at the man in question, wolfing down his bacon, sausages and eggs—she could run more effective anti-abuse programmes at the high school. The two of them could do interactive role plays about appropriate and inappropriate behaviour—something she was sure the kids would enjoy, and if they enjoyed it, they would maybe consider the message.

The man wasn't staying.

And toasted cheese and tomato sandwiches were really, really boring.

'Tell me about the refuge while I eat.'

It *had* been on her mind, well, sort of, so it was easy to talk—easier than thinking right now...

'It began with a death—a young woman who had come to live in the Cove with her boyfriend who was a keen surfer. They hired an on-site van in the caravan park and had been here about three months when the man disappeared and a few days later the woman was found dead inside the van.'

Her voice was so bleak Cam immediately understood that the woman's death had had a devastating effect on Jo Harris.

But doctors were used to death to a certain extent, so this must have been more traumatic than usual?

Why?

'Did you know her?' he asked. 'Had she been a patient?'

Jo nodded.

'No and yes. I'd seen her once—turned out she'd been to the hospital once as well. Perhaps if she'd come twice to me, or gone to the hospital both times...'

He watched as she took a deep breath then lifted her head and met his eyes across the table, her face tight with bad memories.

'She came to me with a strained wrist, broken collarbone and bruises—a fall, she said, and I believed her. As you know, if you're falling, you tend to put out a hand to break the fall, and the collarbone is the weak link so it snaps. Looking back, the story of the fall was probably true but if I'd examined her more closely I'd probably have seen bruising on her back where he'd pushed her before she fell.'

Cam stopped eating. Somehow he'd lost his enjoyment of the huge breakfast. He studied the woman opposite him and knew that in some way she was still beating herself up over the woman's death—blaming herself for not noticing.

'And when she was found in the van? She'd been battered to death?'

Jo nodded.

'I don't think I've ever felt such...' She paused and he saw anguish in her face so wasn't entirely surprised when she used the word.

'Anguish—that's the only way to describe it.

Guilt, too, that I hadn't helped her, but just total despair that such things happen.'

He watched as she gathered herself together—literally straightening her shoulders and tilting her chin—moving onward, explaining.

'After she was dead some of the permanent residents at the park told the police they'd heard raised voices from the van but, like most domestic situations, no one likes to interfere. Her parents came up to the Cove and we found out they'd known he was abusive. In fact, he'd moved up here because she had often sought refuge with her parents and he'd wanted to isolate her even more. They offered a donation—a very generous donation—for someone to set up a refuge here. I...'

She looked out to sea, regret written clearly on her face.

'It was as if I'd been given a reprieve. I might not have been able to help one woman, but surely I could help others. My friend Lauren, a psychologist, had just returned home to work at the Cove and together we got stuck into it, finding out all we could, bringing in people who could help, getting funding for staff.'

She offered him a rueful smile before adding,

'Getting the house turned out to be the easy part.' Then she sighed and the green eyes met his, studying him as if checking him out before telling him any more.

Had he passed some test that she continued, her voice low and slightly husky, as she admitted, 'My sister had just died so, in a way, setting up the refuge helped me, too.'

She smiled but the smile could certainly not be classified as perky, as she admitted, 'It became a passion.'

'And?' he prompted, for he was sure there was more.

One word but it won a real smile—one that lit her eyes with what could only be pride in what she and her friend had achieved, although there were still shadows in them as well. Of course there would be shadows—the memory of the woman who died, then the connection with her sister's death.

A sister who'd loved roses?

He brought his mind back from the roses and shadows in eyes as Jo was talking again.

'Isn't there a saying—build it and they will come? Well, that's what happened with the refuge. It's sad it happened—that places like it are needed—but on the up side, at least now women at risk anywhere within a couple of hundred miles' radius have somewhere to go. I'm connected to it in that I'm on the committee that runs it, and also we, by which I mean the practice, are the medical clinic the women staying there use. Problem is, to keep the refuge open we need ongoing funding from the government to pay the residential workers and that's a bit up in the air at the moment. The powers that be keep changing the rules, requiring more and more measurable 'objectives' in order to attract funding, but...'

She nodded towards his plate. 'This is spoiling your breakfast. Some time soon we'll visit the house and you can talk to Lauren, who runs it, and you can see for yourself.'

Cam returned to his breakfast but his mind was considering all he'd heard. He could understand how personal the refuge must be to Jo, connected to the woman who'd died, as well as to her sister. In a way it was a memorial—almost sacred—so she'd be willing to do anything to keep it going. Even before she'd admitted that the refuge had become a passion he'd heard her passion for it in her voice and seen it in her gleaming eyes as she'd talked about it.

Passion! Hadn't it once been *his* driving force? Where, along the way, had he lost his?

In the battlefields, of course, treating young men so badly damaged many of them wished to die. Dealing with their minds as well as their bodies. No wonder he'd lost his passion.

Except for surfing. *That* passion still burned...

He brought his mind back to the conversation, rerunning it in his head. He found the thing that puzzled him, intrigued in spite of his determination not to get too involved.

'How would employing a middle-aged female doctor in the practice help save the refuge?'

He won another smile. He liked her smiles and was beginning to classify them. This one was slightly shamefaced.

'It wouldn't do much in measurable objectives,' she admitted, 'but it does bother me, personally, that some of the older women who use the house—women in their forties and fifties—might look at Lauren and me and wonder what on earth we could know about their lives or their problems, or even about life in general. I'm twenty-nine so it's not as if I'm fresh out of uni, but I look younger and sometimes I get the impression that the older women might think that though I've got all the theory—'

'Theory isn't reality?'

He couldn't help it. He reached out and touched her hand where it rested on the table.

'Look, I don't know you at all, but having spent just a couple of hours in your company I'm sure you're empathetic enough to be able to see those women's situations through their eyes. The army's the same—a fifty-year-old colonel having to come and talk to some young whippersnapper straight out of med school about his erection problems.'

He paused, then asked, 'I take it you have staff at the refuge?'

The tantalising green eyes studied him for a moment, puzzling over the question.

'We have a number of trained residential support staff, who work with the women all the time.'

'Then surely at least one of them could be an older woman, maybe more than one. These are the people spending most time there.'

Jo nodded.

'You're right, of course. And a couple of them are older women, it's just that…'

'Just that you want to be all things to all people?

No matter how much you do, you always want to do more, give more?'

His new boss stared at him across the table. He could almost see the denial forming on her lips then getting lost on the way out.

'Are you analysing me?' she demanded instead. 'Showing off your psychology skills? Anyway, I don't think that's the case at all.'

He grinned at her.

'You just want the best for everyone,' he offered helpfully, finding pleasure in this gentle teasing—finding an unexpected warmth from it inside his body.

'And what's wrong with that?' she asked, but the words lacked heat and Cam smiled because he knew he'd hit home. She *did* want the best for everyone, she *would* give more and more, but would that be at the expense of her own life? Her own pleasure?

And if so, why?

Intriguing…

Not that he'd ever find out—or needed to. He wasn't looking to stay in Crystal Cove, unexpected warmth or no.

Although…

'Hospital next,' Jo announced, mainly to break

the silence that had followed their conversation, though the man mountain had been demolishing the rest of his breakfast so he probably hadn't found the silence as awkward as she had. She replayed the conversation in her head, realising how much of herself she'd revealed to a virtual stranger.

She'd forced herself to sound bright and cheery as she'd made the 'hospital next' suggestion, but the conversation about the refuge had unsettled her so badly that what she really needed was to get away from Fraser Cameron and do some serious thinking.

Did she really think she could be all things to all people?

Surely she knew that wasn't possible.

So why…?

She concentrated on sounding positive.

'Tom Fletcher, the doctor in charge, lives in a house beside the hospital so if he's not on the wards, I can show you through then take you across to his place to introduce you.'

'Tom Fletcher? Tall, thin guy, dark hair, has women falling over themselves to go out with him?'

Jo frowned at the man who was pushing his

plate away with a sigh of satisfaction. No need to keep worrying about sounding positive when she had a challenge like this to respond to.

'Women falling over themselves to go out with him? What is it with you men that you consider something like that as part of a physical description?'

Her crankiness—and she'd shown plenty—had absolutely no effect on the man who was grinning at her as he replied.

'I knew a bloke of that name at uni—went through medicine with him—and to answer your question, when you're a young, insecure, very single male student you remember the guys who seem able to attract women with effortless ease. I bet you ask another ten fellows out of our year and you'd get the same description.'

Jo shook her head.

'The male mind always was and still remains a total mystery to me,' she said, 'but, yes, Tom is tall and thin—well, he'd probably prefer lean—and has dark hair.'

'Great!'

Cam's enthusiasm was so wholehearted Jo found herself asking if they'd been good friends.

Although if they had, surely Cam would have known his mate was living at the Cove.

'Not close friends, but he was someone I knew well enough. It will be good to catch up with him.'

Would it? Even as he'd spoken, Cam had wondered about 'catching up' with anyone he'd known from his past. Could he play the person he'd been before his war experiences? Could he pretend well enough for people not to see the cracks beneath the surface?

PTSD they called it—post-traumatic stress disorder. He had seen enough of it in patients to be reasonably sure he didn't have it, not the full-blown version of it anyway. All he had was the baggage from his time in the war zone, baggage he was reasonably certain he could rid himself of in time.

Perhaps.

His family had seen the difference in him and understood enough to treat him not like an invalid but with gentleness, letting him know without words that they were all there for him if ever he wanted to talk about the baggage in his head.

Not that he could—not yet—maybe not ever…

Fortunately, before he could let too many of the

doors in his head slide open, his boss was talking to him.

'Come on, then,' she said, standing up and heading across the footpath towards the road. 'It's time to do some catching up.'

'We haven't paid,' he reminded her, and she threw him a look over her shoulder. He considered running the look through his mental data base of women's looks then decided it didn't really matter what her look had said. Best he just followed along, took orders like a good soldier, and hoped he'd prove indispensable so he could stay on in Crystal Cove for longer than a couple of months.

The thought startled him so much he found the word *why* forming in his head.

He tried to answer it.

The surf was good, but there was good surf to be had along thousands of miles of coastline.

Surely not because of the feisty boss—a woman he'd barely met and certainly didn't know, and quite possibly wouldn't like if he did know, although those eyes, the creamy skin...

He reached her as she was about to step out to cross the esplanade, just in time to grab her arm and haul her back as a teenager on a moped swerved towards her.

'Idiot!' Jo stormed, glaring full tilt at the departing rider's back. 'They rent those things out to people with no more brains than a—'

'An aardvark?' Cam offered helpfully, trying not to smile at the woman who was so cross she hadn't realised he was still holding her arm.

He wasn't going to think about *why* he was still holding her arm—he'd just enjoy the sensation.

'I was going to say flea,' she muttered as she turned towards him, 'then I thought maybe I'd said that earlier.' She frowned up at him. 'Why would you think I'd say aardvark?'

He had to laugh.

'Don't you remember telling me I probably had the counselling skills of an aardvark earlier today?'

Her frown disappeared and her cheeks turned a delicate pink.

'How *rude* of me! Did I really?'

She was so obviously flustered—again—he had to let her off the hook.

'I didn't mind,' he told her. 'In fact, I was too astonished to take offence. I mean, it's not ever day one's compared to such an unlikely animal.'

Jo knew she had to move.

For a start, she should shake the man's hand off her arm, but she was mesmerised, not so much by the quirky smile and sparkling blue eyes and the tanned skin and the massive chest but by the fact that she was having such a— What kind of conversation was it?

Light-hearted chit-chat?

It seemed so long since she'd done light-hearted chit-chat, if that's what it was, with a man she didn't know, but whatever it was, she'd been enjoying it…

'Are we going to cross the road or will we stay on this side, discussing aardvarks and fleas?'

Far too late, Jo moved her arm so the man's hand fell off it, then she checked both ways—she didn't want him saving her again—and hurried across, beeping open the car as she approached it, so she could escape inside it as quickly as possible.

Except he'd be getting in as well—no escape.

Until they heard the loud crash, and the sounds of splintering glass.

Cam reacted first, pushing her behind him, looking around, apparently finding the scene of the accident before she'd fully comprehended what had happened.

'It's the moped driver,' he said, as he hurried back across the street to where people were already gathering on the footpath.

Jo followed, seeing the splintered glass of the shopfront and the fallen moped, its wheels still turning, the young driver lying motionless beside it.

'Let's all step back,' Cam said, his voice so full of authority the onlookers obeyed automatically, and when he added, 'And anyone without shoes on, walk away carefully. The glass could have spread in all directions.'

That got rid of a few more onlookers and made Jo aware *she* had to tread carefully. Sandals were fine in summer, but as protection against broken glass not sensible at all.

Cam was kneeling by the young man, who wasn't moving or responding to Cam's questions.

'Unconscious?' she asked, as she squatted on the other side of him, their hands touching as they both felt for injuries.

'Yes, but he's wearing a helmet and the bike barely hit the window before he came off.'

Jo lifted the youth's wrist automatically and

though she was looking for a pulse she had to push aside a metal bracelet. Remembering the rider's swerve earlier, she checked it.

'He's a diabetic,' she said to Cam. 'Maybe he was feeling light-headed when he nearly ran into me. He might have been pulling over to take in some carbs when he passed out.'

'His pulse is racing, and he's pale and very sweaty—I'd say you've got it in one, Dr Harris,' Cam agreed. 'I don't suppose you have a syringe of glucogen on you?'

'I'd have tablets in my bag in the car, but he should have something on him.' She began to search the patient's pockets, pulling out a sleeve of glucose tablets.

Perhaps because she'd been poking at him, their patient stirred.

'That's a bit of luck! I've seen before how blood glucose can rise back to pre-unconsciousness levels,' Cam said, as he helped the young man into a sitting position and asked him if he was able to take the tablets, but Jo had already sent one of the audience to the closest café for some orange juice.

Their patient nodded, muttering to himself about stupidity and not stopping earlier.

The juice arrived and Cam supported him, holding the bottle for the shaky young patient.

'This will be easier to get into you than the tablets,' he said, 'but even though you're conscious you should take a trip up to the hospital and get checked out.' He nodded towards the ambulance that had just pulled up. 'Here's your lift.'

'But the moped?'

'I'll take care of that,' Jo told him. 'I can put it in the back of my vehicle and take it back to the hire people and explain.'

Cam stood back to let the ambulance attendants ready their patient for transport, and looked at Jo, eyebrows raised.

'*You'll* put it in the car?'

He was smiling as he said it, and all kinds of physical symptoms started up again—ripples, flickers, flutters, her skin feeling as if a million tiny sparks were going off inside it.

'Someone would help!' she retorted, trying really hard not to sound defensive but losing the battle.

His smile broadened and now her reactions were *all* internal—a squeezing in her chest, accelerated heartbeat while her lungs suddenly needed all of her attention to make them work.

How could this be happening to her?

And *why*?

Wasn't she perfectly happy with her life?

Well, she was worried about the refuge, but apart from that...

CHAPTER THREE

JO WATCHED the patient being loaded into the ambulance, then turned and spoke to the young policeman who'd arrived, introducing him to Cam, who explained what he'd seen of the incident. While some of the onlookers who'd been closer to the scene gave their versions of what had happened and the shopkeeper began cleaning up the glass, Cam had set the moped upright, and was looking at it, obviously checking for damage.

'I'll handle that, mate,' a voice said, and Jo turned to see that the man who hired out the little motor scooters had arrived with his ute, having heard of the accident on whatever grapevine was in operation this Sunday.

'So, hospital?' Cam asked, once again taking Jo's arm, and although she knew full well it was only to guide her across the street—a street she'd crossed without guidance for a couple of decades—the stirrings in her body magnified and all she wanted to do was get away from him for a short time, give her body a good talking to and move on without all this physical disturbance before it drove her mad.

'I guess so,' she muttered, with so much reluctance Cam halted on the kerb to look at her.

'You've changed your mind about visiting the hospital?'

Was her expression such a giveaway that he added a second question?

'Or changed your mind about employing me?'

Cam watched the woman as he spoke. He was teasing her—well, he was almost certain he was teasing her. It was just that for a moment he thought he'd read regret in her expression.

But he hadn't started work so surely she couldn't be regretting hiring him already.

As if he could read the face of a woman he barely knew! Yes, he could guess at his sisters' emotions, but he'd never really been able to tell what his ex-fiancée was thinking just from looking at her face.

'Why would you think that!' the woman he'd questioned demanded, stepping off the kerb so he was forced to move if he wanted to keep hold of her arm. 'I was thinking of the kid—the diabetic.

It's one of the worries when the schoolies are here, that any kid who is a diabetic can drink too much, or play too hard, and not take in enough fluids. I haven't had an instance here, but that lad made me think.'

That was a very obvious evasion, Cam guessed, but he didn't say so. Whatever Jo *had* been thinking about was her business, not his, although he did hope she wasn't regretting hiring him before he'd even started work.

And it was probably best not to consider *that* hope too closely—could it be more than the surf that made him want to stay on here?

It *couldn't* be the woman—they'd barely met...

And it *certainly* wasn't the accommodation!

Although thinking about waking in the rose bower did make him smile: waking up in the flat would certainly be a far cry from a desert camouflage tent.

But even as he smiled he wondered if he shouldn't leave right now, before he got as entangled as the roses in the bower. It wouldn't be fair to any woman to be lumbered with him the way his mind was—the nightmares, the flashbacks, the doubts that racked him.

Jo beeped the car unlocked, then looked at Cam in vague surprise as opened her door and held it.

'Not used to gentlemen in Crystal Cove?' he asked, discovering that teasing her was fun, particularly as a delicate rose colour seeped into her cheeks when he did it.

Jo refused to answer him. Okay, so he was a tease. She could handle that. She just had to get used to it and to take everything he said with the proverbial grain of salt. *And* she had to learn not to react.

Not to react to *anything* to do with the man.

Already she was regretting suggesting she show him around.

She pulled into the hospital car park, enjoying, as she always did, the old building with its wide, sheltered verandas and its view over the beach and the water beyond.

Today must have been 'putting up the decorations' day for the veranda railing was garlanded with greenery while red and green wreaths hung in all the windows.

'Great hospital!' Cam said.

'It's a triumph of local support over bureaucracy,' she told him. 'The government wanted to close it some years ago and the local people fought to keep it. We've even got a maternity ward, if you can call one birthing suite and a couple of other rooms a ward. It's so good for the local women to be able to have their babies here, and although we don't have a specialist obstetrician we've got a wonderful head midwife, and Tom's passionate about his obstetrics work.'

'I vaguely remember him being keen on it during our training,' Cam said, while Jo hurried out of the car before he could open her door and stand near her again.

She really needed to get away—needed some time and space to sort out all the strange stirrings going on in her body, not to mention the fact that her mind kept enjoying conversations with her new employee. It was almost as if it had been starved of stimulation and was now being refreshed.

Impossible.

Was she away with the fairies that she was even thinking this way?

She was saved from further mental muddle by Tom, who was not only at the hospital, checking on the moped driver, but was delighted to meet up with a friend from bygone times.

'I'm sure you've got better things to do than

hang around listening to us play "Remember this",' Tom told Jo. 'How about you leave Cam here and I'll drop him back up at your place later?'

Jo's relief was out of all proportion to the offer Tom had made, but she hoped she hid it as she checked that this was okay with her new tenant and made her escape.

He was just a man—Cam, not Tom, although Tom was also a man, though not a man she thought of as a *man*.

This particular dither was so ridiculous it told her just how far out of control her mind had become. She drove home, made herself a cup of tea—very soothing, tea—and sat on the deck to try to sort out what was happening to her.

Was it because it was a long time since she'd been in a relationship that her new employee was causing her problems?

Three years, that's how long it had been.

There'd been the odd date in that time—very odd, some of them—but nothing serious. Nothing serious since Harry had declared that no power on earth would persuade him to live in a one-horse, seaside town for the rest of his life, and if she wanted to leave Sydney and go back home, that was fine by him.

He'd been so underwhelmed by her departure from their relationship she'd wondered if he'd already had a replacement woman lined up.

Not that she'd wondered for long. So much had happened after she'd returned home. Jill's death within a few months, for a start. Jo had been devastated. Fortunately she'd had the distraction of helping Lauren set up the refuge, then her father had fallen in love, then she'd taken over the practice. More recently, she'd started worrying about the refuge closing. A new relationship had been the last thing on her mind.

Not that the town was teeming with men with whom she could have had a relationship if she'd wanted one, and relationships in small towns— well, they had their own set of problems.

She was aware enough to know that the refuge, building it up and working for it, had helped her through the worst of the pain of Jill's death. Perhaps now that there was a possibility of it closing, was she subconsciously looking for a new diversion?

A six-foot-three, broad-chested, blue eyed diversion?

She didn't think so.

Besides, the refuge wasn't going to close, not while she had breath in her body to fight it.

And if she *was* fighting, then she wouldn't—shouldn't—have the time or energy to consider her new tenant, not his chest, or his eyes, or anything else about him…

'Who are those people who arrange marriages in some countries? Wedding planners? Marriage consultants?'

It was a strange conversation to be having with someone she barely knew, but Jo was glad the man—the one with the eyes and chest she was going to ignore, however hard that might be—had brought up a topic of conversation for, when she'd met him in the lunch-room after morning surgery, she'd wondered what on earth they could talk about.

They could talk about patients, of course, but lunchtime was supposed to be a break and unless something was urgent—

She frowned at the man, well, not at him but at not knowing the answer.

'I've no idea,' she said, 'although I do know the kind of people you mean. An old-fashioned form of internet dating, I suppose. I think the family went to the woman and she organised the—matchmakers, that's what they were called. Or are called if they still exist.'

She was intrigued enough by now to actually look at the man who was sitting across the table from her. His face was freshly shaven so quirky lips and pale blue eyes were clearly visible, and his hair, though still long, was shiny clean—brown streaked with gold.

He was more handsome even than his photo, which had made him look formal and a little stern, while this man would have every woman in town booking in for appointments.

Best to stop considering his looks and get back to the conversation.

'Why do you ask?'

He grinned at her, making her forget her decision to stop considering looks just long enough to add super-smile to the catalogue of his appeal.

It also caused just a little tremor in her stomach.

Well, maybe more than a *little* tremor, but it was still small enough to ignore.

'Just that every patient I've seen this morning, the men included, would find it a perfect career choice. Some were more subtle than others, but before I'd written a script, every one of them knew my marital status—single—my career prospects—doubtful at present, although most assured me you'd keep me on—and had asked what I thought about my boss. Didn't I think she was a wonderful woman? I've also been told that you're a good cook, one woman seemed to think you could sew, while several others assured me you were a good financial prospect as you owned the surgery and the house and also had investment properties in the city.'

'Sew?'

Cam smiled again as the word burst from his boss's lips.

'Why the hell would anyone be telling you I can sew? Why would I *want* to sew? Why would you be interested? You've been in the army. I'm sure you're much better at sewing than I am, given the number of buttons you must have had on your uniforms, or are doctors the kind of officers who have people who sew on their buttons?'

Knowing all three of his sisters would have reacted with the same horror, Cam continued to smile.

'I think that particular patient thought it was a

nice womanly trait to point out to me, and, no, no button sewers in my army life.'

'You're enjoying this!'

The accusation was accompanied by a fairly good glare, well up on the glare scale he'd set up in his head many years ago. She looked good glaring, too, fiery colour in her cheeks, her eyes seeming greener, a bit like an angry elf.

'Of course,' he said smoothly, teasing her because it was fun. 'Though I do wonder what it is about you that makes everyone think you're incapable of finding yourself a man and that you need help from the whole town to sort out your life.'

A very angry elf!

'Bloody town!' she muttered. 'Honestly, they never let up. I shouldn't have employed you—I knew that right from the start—now we're going to have to put up with every patient casting sideways glances at us, or, as you've found this morning, asking straight out. If I'd had an ounce of sense I'd have come home from Sydney as a widow.'

'Having killed off your husband and got away with it?'

Only with difficulty was Cam holding in a laugh.

'There's no reason I *couldn't* have killed off some mythical husband while I was training in Sydney. Not murdered the poor man, but I could have had him die a painful, lingering death, leaving me grieving for ever. That way they'd have accepted I wasn't interested in a relationship. But coming up here single? Big mistake! I've had patients trailing their sons and nephews and even grandsons through the door—here's Edward in from the farm to meet you, he's got one hundred and forty breeding sows and good teeth. The place is impossible.'

Cam *had* to smile, but just to tease her further he did the maths.

'One hundred and forty breeding sows? What? A couple of litters a year? Twelve to fifteen a litter? Edward would have been a good catch!'

'Edward was not the slightest bit interested in me once he realised I haven't a clue about pork, ham and bacon, and have never known which bit comes from where. What's more, he's happily engaged to a woman who works in the piggery for him, who understands percentage body fat and other things important to pigs.'

Jo hoped she'd spoken coolly enough to put a stop to this absurd conversation, but inside her there was a little glow at the simple pleasure of having someone to talk to, to joke with, while she took a break. Not that she didn't talk and joke to the other staff, two nurses and the receptionist, but talking to Cam was different somehow.

Because he was a man?

Hell's teeth, she did hope not! Her mind went into panic mode at the thought. She didn't know if she was ready for a relationship with a man— well, she was, her body was—but was she ready for the fallout when he moved on? For the talk around the town, for the pain if she was foolish enough to fall in love with him?

Her body's reaction to him could be explained. That was definitely because he was a man, and possibly because her body had been pure and chaste for so darned long she could barely re-member what attraction was like.

Until now.

Though surely it hadn't always been this strong—this immediate…

And how could she be thinking of a relationship when the man had shown not the slightest interest in her as anything other than his boss?

'Mrs Youngman.'

He was looking at her, obviously awaiting a response, his eyes looking grey-blue today—the charcoal shirt?

'I'm sorry, miles away,' she muttered, feeling heat rise in her cheeks when she realised just where her thoughts had been. 'You were saying?'

'Mrs Youngman was one of my first patients. The note on the front of her file said, "Query IVF." She's fifty-two. Has she talked to you about this?'

The question brought Jo's focus back to work immediately.

'Helene Youngman? That's who you're talking about?'

Cam nodded, which didn't help at all.

'Query IVF? Who wrote that?'

Now he shrugged, the impossibly wide shoulders lifting the neat charcoal shirt, moving the material so she saw the V of tanned chest beneath the unbuttoned collar. Nope, her mind might be focussed but her body was still hanging in on the attraction stuff, stirring deep down.

'I've no idea,' he replied. 'I thought maybe you had at her last appointment, or perhaps the receptionist when Mrs Youngman phoned for an appointment.'

'Helene Youngman!' Jo repeated, trying to come to terms with the town's mayor making enquiries about IVF. She had grown-up children and *she* was a widow. Hauling her mind back to work, Jo added, 'She must have asked to see you, to see the new doctor—everyone in town would have known you were here within hours—because she didn't want to talk to me about it, which is a bit of a downer for me as we're quite friendly. Not that it matters who she talks to, of course, but what did you tell her?'

'Only what I knew—specialist clinics in the capital cities, maybe in large regional cities—best to see a gynaecologist first and get checked out before spending too much money. I want to check out information about available programmes so I know for the future, but didn't want to ask one of the nurses because she, Mrs Youngman, gave the impression she was embarrassed enough asking about it, although she must have mentioned it to someone because of the note. I said I'd see what I could find out for her and post it.'

'*Embarrassed?* Poor thing, that's exactly what she would be. Actually, it's hard to believe she came here to enquire, rather than drive down the coast to Port, but she's a busy woman. She's our local mayor and runs two hairdressing salons as well. Although if she goes through with it— and good luck to her if she does—speaking to a doctor about it is going to be the easy part. Facing the local population as it becomes obvious, that's what will be hard for her. We'll need to make sure she gets plenty of support.'

He liked the 'we', as if she'd already accepted him as a colleague, but watching her Cam could practically see Jo's mind working as she tried to puzzle out the request so when she added, 'I didn't even know she was seeing someone, let alone involved enough to want a child with him,' he wasn't surprised to see a blush rise in her cheeks.

She pressed her hands against them.

'What a small-minded thing to say—why *should* I know? That's just what I was talking about earlier. Small-town mentality, you see. We all think we know everything that's going on all the time, and if we don't we're surprised, even a little put out. That's terrible, isn't it?'

The clear green eyes, like the shallow water at the edge of the ocean when the surf was flat, met his with a plea for—understanding? Absolution?

The first he could give.

'It's natural enough, and part of the charm of small towns.' The colour was fading from her cheeks so he went for the second as well. 'And I didn't find it small-minded. To me you simply sounded caring.'

She smiled at him and it was as if the sun had hit the placid green water, sparking golden lights in it.

Golden lights on placid waters? Was his success in getting a job here—even if it was only temporary—turning him fanciful? Had waking up to that spectacular view then the chance for an hour in the surf before breakfast and work altered the chemistry in his brain?

He brought his mind back to work.

'So, what do you know of it? Do you keep information? Is there a specialist clinic in Port Macquarie or would she have to go to Sydney?'

The eyes she fixed on him were serious now, intent, and a little frown was tugging at her eyebrows.

'I've read something recently about some IVF clinics restricting treatment to women over, I think, forty-three. It can't be a totally random age choice but apparently the odds of conception in women older than that are so low they only allow one try.'

'Is that fair?' Cam asked. 'Given the range of ages at which women can reach menopause depending on genetic and other issues, might not a fit fifty-two-year-old woman be as good a recipient of treatment as a younger woman with less healthy reproductive organs?'

Jo smiled at him.

'You'd be wasted surfing along the coast and not working,' she said. 'You're obviously an empathetic doctor and, yes, you're right, it seems strange to pick an age, but funding—it always comes back to money. Check out what you can on the net, ask one of the nurses to dig out the information we have—they won't talk—and we'll take it from there.'

He liked the 'we' part, again, which was foolish given it was his first day at work and the job was temporary. And he'd have liked to talk some more—not necessarily about IVF—but his boss was on her feet, small, neat feet clad in sandals, her toenails painted the palest pink with what looked like little faces or maybe flowers stuck on them.

And since when had he noticed feet? Could

he blame the army and its predilection for shiny boots?

Or could he put that down to the view and early morning surf as well?

'Patients await,' she added as she bustled through the door, although it seemed to him she was escaping something rather than hurrying towards something.

Escaping him?

Was it the small compliment he'd paid her—calling her caring was hardly world-shattering, Jo wondered as she fled the lunchroom. Or was it the attraction that was getting harder to ignore whenever she was near him?

He was just a man.

Okay, he was a tall and handsome man with a chest a gorilla would have been proud of, but physical attributes had never been that important to her in a man. Men she'd loved, well, nearly loved, or thought she'd loved at one time or another hadn't been exactly weedy, but given that she was hardly red-carpet material herself, she'd never expected too much in the way of looks in a man. She'd found attraction in common interests, shared jokes and a sense of being at ease with the person.

And, for some unknown reason, she had been at ease almost from the start with Fraser Cameron, even when she'd thought he might be coming to rob the surgery.

She had to get her head straight.

Think about Helene! She was healthy—kept herself fit running and swimming—in fact, Jo often ran with her on the beach in the early mornings.

And she wanted a baby?

A totally unfamiliar sensation coiled in Jo's belly.

No! No way was she going to get clucky now! She *never* got clucky. She handled babies every day of the week and heard not even the faintest tick of the fabled clock.

Because she'd never fancied anyone enough to get involved, enough to consider having children with him?

Even Harry?

That was a scary thought because it prompted the question why now, and she didn't want to consider the answer in case it had something to do with blue eyes and a quirky smile and soft brown hair with gold highlights…

It took some effort, but she turned her mind back to work matters.

She collected the pile of files for her afternoon appointments and headed into her room, promising herself she'd do some research into IVF for older women on the internet later. It would keep her busy after dinner which was good because the previous night, imagining Cam in the flat next door, had been so uncomfortable she'd ended up going back to the beach and running until she was exhausted enough to go home and sleep.

Maybe a bit of IVF research would be good...

And the squirmy feeling in her stomach was probably indigestion.

Fate dictated that her first three patients of the afternoon were babies. Two were in for injections, which one of the nurses would give, and six-month-old Kaylin, a gurgling bundle of delight had decided she didn't need to sleep.

Ever!

'She's okay now because she's been in the car and she always sleeps in the car,' Kaylin's mother, Amy Bennett, explained. 'But we can't drive around all night so she gets some sleep because it means we don't get any. We're getting desperate, Jo, and Todd gets so cranky when he doesn't get his sleep and I know I'll lose my milk if things don't settle down. With the dairy we can't avoid the milking every morning and with a hundred milkers Todd needs my help. In the beginning Kaylin was good, she'd just sleep in the capsule down at the dairy while we worked, but that only lasted about a month. Remember I came in to talk to you before...'

Amy's voice trailed away.

Jo thought about it as she dug through files in the cabinet behind her for information on the sleep programme offered from time to time at the local hospital in conjunction with various government departments.

Any number of babies had problems developing regular sleep patterns, but Kaylin had so far defied all the tried and trusted methods of training babies to sleep and not only was Amy looking stressed and worn out, but the baby, too, was suffering.

Think laterally! Jo reminded herself of her father's words. Running a successful practice in a small coastal town meant understanding the dynamics of her patients' lives. A pregnant woman with complications might refuse to go to the more specialised hospital in the nearest regional city unless someone—usually the family doctor—organised someone to look after her older children.

She'd learnt this from her father even before she studied medicine, hearing him discuss options for patients' welfare that went beyond straight doctoring.

So as far as sorting things out for Amy went, Kaylin's sleeping pattern was only part of the problem.

'I can arrange for you to stay at the hospital while the expert works with you and Kaylin,' Jo explained as Amy leafed through the information, 'but it means Todd will have to get someone in to give him a hand with the milking. You've still got that old house on the property, haven't you? The one you've rented out from time to time?'

Amy nodded.

'Then maybe you could offer it rent free to someone in exchange for help with the milking. That will give you more time to spend with Kaylin. Now she's getting too big for the capsule, you'd have to find an alternative way to keep her safe while you're helping Todd, in any case.'

Amy looked doubtful.

'You know we did it once before,' she murmured. 'I think it was your dad, just before he left, that arranged for the Scott family to have the house.'

'Oh, dear, not so good a suggestion, then,' Jo replied, remembering the complicated plan she and Lauren had cooked up to get Mrs Scott and the two little Scotts out of the house and into the recently opened refuge when the man Todd Bennett had employed had turned out to be an abusive husband.

Jo shuddered at the memory, thinking of the volunteer who'd driven the wife and children to safety and who had later been targeted by Bob Scott. The volunteer's house had been peppered with eggs and tomatoes.

'But then again, it's hardly likely you'd get another couple like the Scotts.'

Amy shrugged.

'You just don't know, do you?' she said, but after Jo had checked out both her and Kaylin, Amy agreed she'd talk to Todd about it and let Jo know if she wanted to stay in the hospital for the sleep programme.

'Do you know where Mrs Scott and the kids went?' she asked as Jo was walking with her back to the reception area.

'Back to Mr Scott,' Jo told her, remembering

how wary she'd been when the woman had made that decision. 'Mr Scott completed a programme they were running in Port to help men like him and I think he joined a support group, so hopefully it all worked out.'

Amy waved goodbye and Jo turned to go back to her room to check who was next. She ran smack bang into a broad chest.

'Men like him?' the owner of the chest repeated. 'Abusive?'

Jo nodded, her mind still full of the uneasiness that thinking about the Scotts had caused.

'And the man went to Port? There's a refuge but no programme for men here?'

Jo had backed away from him, and now his persistence forced her to look up into his face.

'The Scotts were gone two years ago, why the interest?'

Cam beamed at her, his smile so warm she felt it radiate against her skin.

And set alarm bells clanging in her head!

'It's something I can do,' he announced, still beaming with delight at whatever he was thinking. 'Something I can set up. If not a regular programme at least a support-slash-discussion group.'

It was an excellent idea, and something she and Lauren had often discussed, but why was Cam being so helpful?

So he'd have to stay on?

'You're only here for a couple of months,' she reminded him.

'On trial for a couple of months.' His retort was so swift she knew he'd followed her thoughts. 'Anyway, if it doesn't work out here at the clinic, I could always stay on in town and surf for a few more months, maybe pick up some shifts at the hospital. Tom said yesterday that they could probably get funding for a part-time doctor, and after the holidays I can live in my van in the caravan park so I wouldn't be bothering you.'

Bothering her?

Had he guessed how she was reacting to him? Well, not her so much but her body...

Whether it was his proximity—the hall was getting narrower by the minute—or the thought of Cam being around for longer than was absolutely necessary, Jo didn't know. All she knew was that she feeling extremely flustered and she *did* know she didn't do flustered.

Ever.

'We've both got patients to see,' she reminded

Cam, and stomped away, even more put out because the soft-soled sandals she wore didn't make satisfactory stomping noises.

Hmm.

Cam watched her go.

Had he flustered her?

Jo Harris didn't strike him as a woman who flustered easily.

And why was he thinking about her—in particular, why was he thinking about her as a woman? He may not have PTSD, but he certainly wasn't in any state to be getting involved with a woman. He couldn't blame Penny for cutting him out of her life, knowing the man who'd returned to her hadn't been the man she'd loved, but if *she* couldn't love the new him, who would?

Remote, she'd called him. Remote, detached, and morose.

He hadn't liked the morose with its undertones of brooding, but the remote bit had really got to him. It was a word that sounded unpleasant. It could never be used to describe Jo. He'd seen her angry, and snappish, and competently assured as she'd knelt by the injured moped driver. He'd even seen the shadows of sadness in her face, but she was always involved—ready with an opinion, seeking new ideas.

Remote suggested a detachment from the world, and for sure it was one of the symptoms of PTSD that he *had* been able to tick. On leaving the army, he'd felt as if the world he'd returned to was a parallel universe and he was rudderless in it. He'd been on the outside, looking in, aware that none of the people around him could, in their wildest dreams, have imagined what he'd seen and been through.

The strange thing was that he didn't feel that way now. Maybe it was the surf at Crystal Cove clearing his head, but the idea of starting a support group had stirred something akin to excitement in him, *and* he was looking forward to doing some research on IVF treatments for older women.

Looking forward to helping people?

Getting involved?

He wasn't sure what had caused the change, but though he might be on the right track he suspected he had a lot more healing to do before he could think in terms of a relationship with a woman.

Although Jo obviously had her own baggage— her sister's death, for a start.

Could two wounded souls somehow help each other heal?

He remembered how her eyes had looked—clear green pools—and his body stirred in a way that was totally inappropriate as a reaction to one's boss, however temporary his employment might be...

CHAPTER FOUR

'I HADN'T realised how much more quickly we'd get through the day with two doctors.'

Jo had been chatting to the receptionist when Cam showed his final patient out. Now she walked with him back along the hall.

'I phoned Lauren, who runs the refuge, earlier. The two families who are living there at the moment are having a "treat night" tonight, which means there's no one at the house. We could go over later if that suits you. You could see the place and talk to Lauren about how it works and also about the men's programme. Funding is always difficult—sometimes impossible. Originally we got the bequest to set up the refuge, but that's not enough to keep it going these days so poor Lauren gets bits and pieces from different government agencies. One of the local service clubs has it as their main charity, but I can't promise you'd be paid for running a men's programme, although if you start it while you're working for me, but then…'

She stopped and looked up at him, a worried frown knitting her eyebrows.

'Of course you don't have to come with me, you might prefer to go surfing or have other stuff you want to do but—'

'Jo!'

Cam held up his hands as he said her name—a placating gesture, not surrender.

'Calm down. We can't change the entire world right now. Let's take it one step at a time. I'm more than happy to go with you to see the refuge, and seeing it when no one's there is an excellent idea. Do I have time for a quick shower and change of clothes before we go?'

She was staring at him, a bewildered look on her face, then he watched as she gathered herself together, shaking her head just slightly as if to get everything back into place.

'I *never* blather on like that!' she said, her tone so accusing he had to laugh.

'Blathering's okay,' he assured her, but the worried look on her face told him she didn't believe him. He diverted her by repeating his question.

'Shower?'

'Of course,' she said, but he guessed it had been an automatic response, her mind still occupied by the blather business.

Jo was glad he'd left as soon as she'd agreed they had time to freshen up, because now, maybe, she could sort out what was happening to her.

The men's programme was an excellent idea, and she had no doubt Cam, with his training and experience, would be just the man to set it up and run it.

And even if the refuge closed, the programme could still run, so it wasn't that disturbing her...

Was it because he'd talked of staying on that she'd been thrown into a dither?

Had she somehow convinced herself that she could put up with the distraction he was causing her body for a couple of months but once the issue of his staying longer had arisen, her brain had gone into meltdown?

She couldn't answer either of her questions so she locked her office door, said good-bye to Kate who was working Reception today, and hurried up the steps at the back of the surgery.

Maybe a shower would help her brain return to normal, but cold or hot she had no confidence in it doing anything to stop her body reacting to her temporary employee.

It was only a couple of months!

But could she let him live in his van in the caravan park if he stayed on to run a men's programme?

She had the flat…

Best not to think ahead.

But for the second day in a row, she put on just a little lipstick.

Pathetic.

The refuge was behind one of Crystal Cove's still functioning churches. It had been the minister's house—the manse—once, but now the minister lived forty miles up the coast and served a flock spread over a wide area, holding services at the Cove once a fortnight.

'It's fairly obvious, isn't it?' Cam asked as Jo pulled into the driveway.

She looked around at the high wire fence, the security cameras at the corners of the old wooden residence, the playground equipment out the back.

Turned back to Cam.

'In what way?'

'Well, I thought they had to be anonymous

places, women's refuges, hidden away—ordinary houses but their use not known even to neighbours.'

Jo smiled at him—he was so darned easy to smile at.

And she'd better think about *that* thought later.

'In bigger towns and cities that might be possible and it's definitely desirable, but in a town this size? As you'd surmised, towns this size don't usually have a refuge. We're lucky because the church not only lets us have the premises rent free, but they pay expenses on it—rates and such. The service clubs did a lot of renovations and they do any maintenance that's required, so immediately you have several groups of people who know where it is and what it's for. And it *is* only two doors from the police station so there's never any trouble here. '

She frowned now as she added, 'Am I blathering again?'

He grinned at her.

'No way. That was a most sensible explanation, very to the point and concise.'

The grin was her undoing. Any good the shower might have done was undone with that grin—a quirky, amused, sharing kind of grin.

Good grief! How could she possibly be thinking this way?

Analysing the man's grin?

'Let's go,' she said, opening her door and leaping down from the high seat of the four-wheel drive that had been her Christmas present to herself last year.

Good thing, too, she thought, patting the car when she'd shut the door. Having Cam in the big vehicle had been bad enough, she could only imagine how uncomfortable it would have been if they'd been squashed together in a small sedan.

Lauren Cooper, blonde, beautiful but far too thin and with dark shadows of worry under her eyes, came out of the house to greet them.

'You have to take some time off,' Jo scolded her best friend.

'I'll have plenty of time off if we have to close,' Lauren reminded her quietly, but her dark eyes lit up as she took in the man Jo was introducing to her.

'Well,' she teased after she'd shaken Cam's hand, 'you'll certainly be a great addition to the male talent in this town.'

'All six of them?' Jo countered.

'In our age group,' Lauren agreed, counting

on her fingers as she listed the local, older, unattached men. 'Mike at the police station, Tom at the hospital, that new schoolteacher—'

'He's got a partner,' Jo protested, before adding firmly, 'Anyway, that's enough. Cam's already likely to get a swollen head because I've been praising his idea of the men's support programme. We're here to see the refuge and to talk about how we could run a men's programme—not to mention whether men might come.'

'It could be court mandated,' Cam offered, pleased the conversation had shifted from male talent in the town. His body might have reacted to his boss and landlady but after Penny's fairly brutal rejection, he'd accepted that until the mess in his head was sorted out, it would be unfair to get involved with any woman.

Although a woman with killer green eyes...

'Wow!'

His exclamation was involuntary, and his mind right back on the refuge as Lauren led them first into what she called the playroom. Obviously it had been set up with kids in mind, but whoever had conceived and carried through the idea had done an amazing job. Blackboard paint had been used to adult waist height on all the walls so there were chalk drawings everywhere. At one end of the long room—a closed-in veranda, he suspected—was a sitting area with comfy armchairs and bean-bags in front of a television set with a DVD player on top of it. Beside that a cabinet held what must be at least a hundred DVDs.

The other end of the room was obviously for very small people, blocks and jigsaw puzzles neatly put away on shelves, plastic boxes of farm animals, zoo animals, dinosaurs, toy cars and little dolls stacked further along the shelves.

'It's incredibly well stocked,' he said, 'and so tidy.'

'Well-stocked but not always so tidy,' Lauren told him. 'We've instituted star charts. Stars for putting away the toys, stars for cleaning teeth, stars for just about everything you can imagine. Once you get a certain number of stars, you get a treat—like dinner at a fast-food outlet of your choice, which is where everyone is tonight. They left early as they're going on to a movie after their meal. Everyone's been really good this week!'

Lauren showed them through the rest of the house, allowing Cam a glimpse into the three big bedrooms that could accommodate up to five people in each.

'So you can have three women with children—
no more?' Cam asked.

'Well, we could arrange to take more if it was
necessary, squeeze in a woman on her own, for
instance, but the turnover is fairly rapid.'

'So no one is here long term?' Cam asked.

Lauren smiled at him, the smile lifting the
tiredness from her face and making him wonder
why this beautiful woman—smiling at him—had
no effect at all on his body, while the small, pert
redhead who was usually frowning, glaring or
arguing did.

Not that he needed to give it much thought—he
was moving on.

And even if he stayed, he'd be moving out.

And then there was the baggage.

And his lost passion…

'Four weeks.'

He'd missed the beginning of whatever Lauren
was saying but assumed she'd told him the time
limit on stays as she led him into the communal lounge, the dining area and finally a well-
equipped kitchen.

'You're really well set up,' he said, not bothering to keep the admiration out of his voice.

'That's what makes the thought of it closing so hard.'

He heard the pain in Jo's voice, but it was the content, not the pain, he had to think about.

'But as long as you're fighting the closure you've got a chance of keeping it open,' he protested. 'I thought it was because of the refuge you were employing another doctor. The fortyish woman, remember.'

He won a slight smile.

'I was employing her—or you—to ease my load at work so I could put more time into this, time for paperwork mainly, applying for grants, and so on. As I told you yesterday, the refuge began with a bequest and the building itself is available to us free of charge, but ongoing funding for residential staff—the people here every day, including the child-healthcare worker—has to come from the government. The government is forever issuing new guidelines and procedures and so-called measurements of success—criteria we have to meet before they'll give us money.'

'Sounds like the army,' Cam said, 'but I thought women being saved from abuse would be counted as successes.'

'You'd think so,' Jo told him, 'but they like

"projects".' She used her fingers to put the word in inverted commas. 'That's why a men's programme would be fantastic, *and* we could do more work in schools. It would be such a waste to have to close it now, when we've come so far.'

She smiled, but it was a weak effort.

'The thing is, we've worked so hard for the women who need us to accept us and on top of that we have the most wonderful local support,' Lauren explained. 'People from all walks of life help out in different ways. The local bakery gives us its unsold bread at the end of each day—not to mention buns and bread rolls. We get a discount at the butcher's and the supermarket, and the fruit shop in town also hands over any produce they aren't able to sell.'

'Which is a blessing,' Jo put in, with a far better smile, this time broad enough to gleam in her eyes, 'given that the back yard has a virtual zoo, with rabbits, guinea pigs, chickens and a duck with one leg that someone gave us. At one stage there was a lamb but it turned into a sheep and the neighbours complained about the noise it made.'

Cam looked at the smiling woman who *did* affect his body and regretted mentioning a programme for abusive men. Much better if he moved on at the end of the holidays. He didn't need to get involved in the problems of the refuge, did he? There were other towns with good surf. In fact, he had thousands of miles of coastline to choose from.

But no snappish, elfin-faced, green-eyed doctor…

'If there's a programme up and running in Port, maybe I could go down and speak to whoever runs it,' he heard a voice say.

He was reasonably sure it was *his* voice.

A buzzing sound made him turn towards the woman he'd been considering, and he watched as she pulled her mobile out of her pocket.

She walked through the back door and spoke quietly, but not so quietly he and Lauren didn't hear her end of the conversation.

'I'll come at once,' she said. 'Pack just what you need, and don't forget any medication and the little bundle of papers that were on the list I gave you. We'll be fifteen minutes getting there, but if you feel unsafe leave the house now—go to a neighbour and phone again from there.'

'New tenant?' Lauren asked as Jo came back into the kitchen.

'Jackie Trent, I talked to you about her.'

Lauren nodded and followed Jo, who was hurrying towards the front door.

It was a case of trailing along behind.

Cam trailed, then four of the words Jo had spoken were suddenly clear in his head.

If you feel unsafe, she'd said.

He stopped trailing and hurried ahead, reaching the passenger side as she clambered in behind the wheel, his presence obviously forgotten.

'I'm coming with you,' he said.

'You don't need to,' she replied, her attention on fastening her seat belt. 'You can stay and have a coffee with Lauren and learn more about the house—talk about the men's programme. I'll collect you later.'

'No, I'll come,' Cam told her, fastening his seat belt in turn.

'She's scared,' Jo said, not arguing exactly as she started the engine, put the vehicle into gear and backed out of the drive.

'I won't scare her more,' Cam assured her, not adding that the woman must have reason to be scared and if she did then Jo, also, should be scared. There was no way he was leaving two scared women with no protection.

'She's talked about leaving for the last six

months,' Jo told him. What she didn't tell him was that in her heart of hearts she was very pleased to have his support on this rescue mission. 'Apparently he'd always arranged every detail of their lives, but Jackie had seen that as part of his love for her, but then, just last year, he hit her. She was pregnant at the time. She fell, and a few hours later she lost the baby. It wasn't necessarily the fall that caused her to miscarry, it could have happened anyway, but the two things were definitely connected in her mind. She was so upset about it she told me about him hitting her...'

'Did you believe it was the first time?' Cam's barely disguised anger at the thought of a man hitting a woman was so genuine Jo put the memory of Jackie's misery out of mind and found a smile. She was only too aware that there was little to smile about right now, but she was pleased her new employee knew enough about abuse to ask the question. Had he always known or was that why the light had been on in the flat until the wee hours of the morning?

Research?

'It might have been, although while she was in hospital overnight—I did a D and C after it—I met him a couple of times. He straightened everything on the bedside cabinet, ordered her dinner for her, and checked his watch when she went to the bathroom. I realised he was keeping himself under rigid control because I was there, but you could tell he ran her life down to the last detail—a totally controlling man.'

She heard Cam sigh, and saw him shake his head.

'From what I've read,' he said, confirming her guess he'd been studying up on it, 'the first thing to do is persuade the men to accept responsibility for their actions. If they can do that, then they can move on to the next step of learning other ways to resolve problems—other ways to handle anger. The depressing thing from my research seems to be that many will never change, is that right?'

'I think a good percentage do, especially those who have ongoing involvement with a group or a mentor,' Jo replied.

'Even though most men blame the women for their reactions?' Cam said. '"It's her fault—she started it" kind of thing.'

Jo smiled.

'You *have* been reading up on it,' she teased.

'Of course,' he said, sounding slightly put out. 'Wouldn't you have expected me to?'

Jo was pulling into Jackie's street, driving slowly, alert for any parked cars or other vehicles approaching.

'Maybe not quite so soon,' she said. 'This is the house. There's no car here but we won't park in the driveway. That's one of the golden rules of a rescue. Don't make it too easy for someone to block you in. Not that there's any great danger. According to Jackie, her husband's gone to indoor cricket so he shouldn't be home for a couple of hours.'

Jo turned off the engine and although she was sure Jackie was right, she still made sure the interior light was off before she opened the door and slid out. The evening was still and strangely silent, and suddenly she was very glad to have Cam as back-up, right there just a pace behind her as she walked up the path.

Jackie was out the door before Jo reached it, hustling her two children in front of her, both of them wearing pyjamas and backpacks, Jackie towing two suitcases.

Crying.

Cam helped the two boys into the back of the big vehicle, detaching them from their backpacks first. He slid the second one into the middle seat, explaining he'd sit in there with them.

'Mum's crying again,' the older one said.

'She'll be okay,' Cam told him. 'Now, let's introduce ourselves. I'm Cam, and you are?'

'Jared,' the older one replied, then he nudged his brother. 'Tell 'im your name, stupid!'

Cam felt the sigh inside him this time. Okay, so it might be normal childish behaviour but the way the little fellow whispered his name, 'Aaron', Cam had to wonder if the culture of abuse had already been passed from father to son—to the elder son at least.

He'd been helping the kids to keep out of Jo's way as she looked after their mother, but now, before getting into the car with the kids, he glanced around. The two women had disappeared.

Cam lifted the two suitcases they'd left behind into the rear compartment, and had shut the tailgate when they reappeared, Jo hustling Jackie down the path.

'But he gets so angry if I leave a light on after I leave a room,' Jackie was explaining, and Cam realised for the first time the hold abuse could have on a person. Here was a woman literally fleeing for her life and she'd gone back into the house to turn off a light to avoid the anger of the man she feared.

The man she was fleeing.

Cam held the door for Jackie, acknowledging Jo's introduction before climbing in the back with the kids.

'Cam's come to work with me,' Jo said, adding, 'over the holidays,' just late enough to give Cam a little hope that the job might turn into something more permanent.

Although if he continued to feel physical disturbances whenever he was around her, maybe the couple of months' trial period would be more than enough.

And he hadn't wanted anything permanent anyway.

Had he?

A slight disturbance beside him took his mind off his boss. Aaron's body was shaking, the little boy in tears.

'Sook!' his brother said, but under his breath so his mother didn't hear.

Aware it wasn't his place to chastise the older boy, Cam settled his arm around the little fellow and drew him close. He'd seen too many children cry, and that quivering little body spiked memories into his heart, hurting it so badly he had to take a deep breath and force his mind back to the present.

What he needed was a diversion.

'Can you swim?' he asked Aaron. 'Do you go to the beach? I'm a surfer and I go there most mornings. Maybe one day, if your mum says its okay, I could take you out on my surfboard.'

'Me too?' Jared demanded, and Cam agreed he could take him as well.

'As long as you're a good boy and look after your little brother.'

He had been going to say 'look after your mum' but remembered just in time something else he'd read the previous evening. According to research children were mostly left alone in domestic abuse situations, unless they tried to protect the person suffering abuse—usually the mother.

'I can swim real well,' Jared told him, while young Aaron snuggled closer, warm against Cam's side, and whispered that he, too, could swim.

Cam's arm tightened around him, the feel of the small body pressed to his warming some of the cold places inside his body.

Inside his heart?

It was always the kids who suffered.

They'd reached the refuge, and Cam was pleased that the 'treat' lot were still out. It would give Lauren time to settle Jackie and the two boys into the vacant room.

'Do we hang around?' he asked Jo, aware now the activity had died down that he was starving. He glanced at his watch—nine o'clock—no wonder.

Jo saw the glance and as her own stomach was grumbling she knew what he was thinking.

'We can go,' she told him. 'In fact, it's best we do. Lauren will settle Jackie in before the others come home.'

She was uncertain what to say next—sure Cam wouldn't have had time to do much shopping and not knowing how much food he could keep in his van. Fortunately he broke the silence.

'Well, it's too late to be cooking dinner,' he told her, 'and I'm fairly short of supplies in the van, so, is there somewhere good we can eat?'

His smile caused what were becoming customary disturbances inside her, and she was about to protest that she'd be fine—after all, he could find himself something to eat—when he spoke again.

'Come on, what's the absolute best place to eat in town?'

'Surf club,' she replied automatically, definitely not thinking things through. Things like eating at the surf club looking out at moonlight on the ocean, with a man to whom she didn't want to be attracted.

'Although it could be closed by now,' she finished, but not quickly enough.

'Closed by now?' Cam echoed. 'It's only nine o'clock!'

He sounded so disbelieving Jo had to smile at him.

'Country hours,' she explained, then to escape, or perhaps to hide the smile that didn't want to go away, she added, 'I'll just let Lauren know we're going.'

She slipped away, relieved to be out of Cam's presence, although she'd been pleased to have it earlier. *And* she was stuck with him for another hour or two, depending on how long it took to order, get served and eat a meal.

Stuck with him and the moon and the ocean…

Perhaps clouds had covered the sky while they'd been inside.

That wish wasn't granted. As she pulled into the

car park she had to acknowledge that it was a near perfect late November evening. The moon—yep, almost full—was shining down on the ocean. The clubhouse, tucked away from southerlies behind the headland, looked north across the bay and out to sea.

Unbelievably beautiful.

Picture-postcard perfect.

Romantic.

How could the sudden advent of one man into her life start her thinking of romance?

Was she so needy? Frustrated? Desperate for love?

Love?

Now, where had that word come from?

CHAPTER FIVE

'NOT much surf,' Cam said, obviously checking out the waves while she was muddling around in her head with moonlight on water and other *most* unsuitable thoughts.

The irony of the situation made her smile. Totally unaware of the effect he was having on her, the man who was confusing her so badly was thinking surf.

She could do surf.

And thinking surf was miles better than thinking romance.

'You should get a southerly swell coming up on the open beach south of the headland over the next few days,' Jo told him, having automatically checked the weather report on the internet before she'd left the surgery.

'You surf yourself?' he asked, touching her on the arm as he asked the question, so she had to stop walking towards the clubhouse and turn to answer him.

'Not any more,' she said, then, before sadness could overwhelm her and spoil the magic of the beautiful evening, she added, 'All the local kids surf almost from the time they can stand up on a surfboard, but it's hardly the most sensible sport for someone with my colouring.'

She'd ducked out of the question a bit too neatly, Cam decided as he followed her into the surf club. She led him not into the downstairs part where all the gear would be kept but up some steps to one side and onto an enclosed veranda where the view was even better than it had been downstairs.

The desire to question her further was almost overwhelming, but even on short acquaintance he was beginning to read her 'keep off' signs and there was definitely one in place right now.

A keep-off sign and a look of sadness on her face. Not unlike the look when she'd walked into the little flat.

Some connection?

He didn't like her looking sad.

Not that he should care, but she *was* his boss.

The restaurant was all but empty, another couple sitting close to the windows on the western side, nodding to Jo who crossed to say hello.

Cam let the young man who'd met them at the

door show him to a table on the opposite side of
the room, a table that gave a spectacular view out
to sea. Jo joined him, explaining the other couple
were regular visitors to the Cove, coming for a
couple of months each year and having their final
dinner for this visit at the club.

'Do you come here often?'

He trotted out the trite pick-up phrase with just
enough amusement in his voice for her to hear it
for what it was, and smile.

'Excellent conversational opening—a little
lacking in originality but full marks for sounding sincere.'

She filled their glasses with water from the
carafe on the table before speaking again.

'To answer truthfully, I wish I could but I never
seem to have time, or when I do have a free evening, I'm usually too tired to be bothered going
out,' she said. 'They do the best calamari if you're
a calamari eater. Other places manage to make it
taste like stethoscope tube but here it's melt-in-
the-mouth-perfect.'

She turned to greet the waiter who'd approached
their table, introducing Cam to the young man.

'He won't be here for long,' she added, and just
as Cam decided he'd had enough of being intro-

duced as a temporary gap-filler he realised she was talking *to* him, not about him. The person who wouldn't be here long was their waiter.

'He's one of the best surfers the Cove has ever produced,' Jo was saying. 'He's off to join the pro tour at the start of next season.'

'I'm not as good as Nat Williams,' the young man said.

'Nat Williams came from Crystal Cove?' Cam demanded, surprised he didn't know that the current legend of world surfing was a local boy.

'Grew up with Jo here,' the young waiter said. 'Everyone said she could have been just as good, but of course…'

He stopped and blushed so the few adolescent spots on his face turned purple.

Had Jo trodden on his foot to stop his revelations?

What revelations?

'And you're having?' the young man asked, startling Cam into the realisation that he hadn't looked at what was on offer, and he wasn't that fussed about calamari, tender or not.

'Perhaps you could get us our drinks while he looks,' Jo suggested in a patently false kindly voice. 'Who knows how long he'll take to choose now he's actually opened the menu?'

Was she taking a swipe at him to divert him from the earlier revelations? He had no idea, and knew it shouldn't matter but why anyone would stop surfing—short of losing a limb to a shark—he couldn't imagine. In his head he'd still be riding the waves when he was eighty.

Ninety?

He *had* to ask.

'You were as good a surfer as Nat Williams? Did you consider the pro circuit? Were you good enough for that?'

She frowned at him, toyed with her glass of water and finally sighed.

'I might have been,' she said, looking away from him, out to the ocean where at some time she must have been totally at home. 'I won junior titles, a few intermediate ones.'

'And you stopped?'

He couldn't keep the incredulity out of his voice, but instead of responding—well, it wasn't really a question—she diverted him by reminding him he was supposed to be studying the menu.

He ordered the fish of the day, feeling it wouldn't be right to be eating steak in a restaurant right on the beach, and sipped the light beer he'd managed to order earlier. And before he could follow up on her surfing past, she diverted him again.

Intentionally?

He had no idea, but it was some diversion.

'You do realise that now you've told those two little boys you'll take them surfing that you'll have to keep your word?' she said.

'I didn't think you'd have heard that conversation,' he replied, to cover his surprise. 'You and Jackie were talking the whole time. But of course I'll keep my word. Poor kids, stuck in a situation like that. It makes me realise just how lucky I was with my childhood. Are they likely to be at the refuge for long?'

Jo shrugged her shoulders, the little movement drawing his attention to her breasts, which lifted at the same time. His mind went haywire—sending him an image of her in a bikini, riding in on a wave, a slight figure but as shapely as a mermaid on the prow of an old sailing vessel.

'It depends on so much,' she was saying. 'She has the option of staying a month, but usually if a woman is serious about not going back to her husband or partner, the organisation has found other accommodation for her before that.'

She studied him for a moment, then asked, 'Would you like me to run through the process?'

Not particularly.

Not right now.

I'd rather know your surfing history...

Those were his answers of choice but his reasoning—he'd rather talk about her—seemed far too, well, invasive at this stage of their involvement, so he nodded.

He also pushed the new door, which was sliding open and revealing totally unnecessary but vividly imagined images of his bikini-clad boss, firmly closed yet again.

'The first thing Lauren will do with Jackie—after they've settled the kids into bed—is sit down with her to make a list of her—Jackie's—priorities. What does *she* want to do? After safety for herself and the children, what's most important for her?'

Totally focussed now, Cam considered this, then asked, 'Will she know?'

Jo smiled. He wasn't stupid, this big hunk of manhood she'd employed—

Temporarily!

'Not immediately but they work on a plan for now—what's most important now. Whenever a

woman talks to us about leaving an abusive relationship we give them all the information we
can—about keeping as safe as possible within
their home until they make the decision to leave,
telling someone else the problem, making sure the
children know a neighbour they can go to, that
kind of thing. We also give them a list of papers
to secure somewhere so they can be grabbed in a
hurry—all the documents all governments insist
we produce in order to prove we are who we say
we are.'

'You mean things like birth certificates?'

Jo nodded.

'And marriage certificates, kids' birth certificates as well, driving licence, bank books or bank
account numbers, medical scripts, although we
can replace those.'

She paused and looked across the table at Cam.
He was so darned good looking she couldn't believe she was sitting here discussing work matters
with him.

Well, actually she could. He was so darned good
looking she doubted he'd ever discuss anything
but work matters with a fairly ordinary-looking
female like herself.

A twinge of what could only be regret ran

through her, then he smiled—an ordinary, encouraging, I'm listening kind of smile—and something very different in the way of twinges rippled down her spine.

It was followed very quickly by a rush of panic.

Attraction was the last thing she needed in her life right now.

Wasn't it?

She had no idea. Perhaps because she hadn't felt it for so long she hadn't given it much thought. She was reasonably sure she hadn't missed having a man in her life.

Well, not enough to worry about it.

'So she has her papers?' he prompted, and Jo blinked and tried really hard to concentrate on the conversation—tried really hard to ignore twinges and ripples and whatever they might mean.

Jackie's papers—that's what they'd been talking about.

'All of them, I hope. If she has no money she can apply for a crisis payment. Actually, Lauren will ask *her* how she might go about getting money—letting her take control right from the start.'

How much to explain?

'One of the reasons women find it hard to leave

their abusers is that they've become dependent on them, so as well as providing a safe place to live, the refuge staff take whatever steps they can to give the women confidence in managing their own affairs. Staff members provide forms and information and can help but the women have to first work out what they want, think about how it might be achieved and then at least begin to get it organised for themselves.'

'With support,' Cam said.

'With whatever level of support they need, and that varies tremendously,' Jo agreed. 'It's all about helping them take control of their lives and mostly they've lost so much control it's very, very difficult for them.'

'Which would make it easier to go back to someone who did all that stuff for them even though he batters them?'

'Exactly!'

She knew she should have let it go at that, but the familiar frustration was building inside her.

'It is *so* exasperating,' she muttered. 'We—well, not me but the support staff at the refuge—can get them so far along the road to independence then suddenly it all becomes too hard and back they go, assuring us all—and themselves—that he, whoever he is, is really, really sorry and he has promised faithfully never to do it again, etcetera, etcetera.'

Her anger was easy to read, sparking in her eyes, colouring her cheeks—the angry elf again but a very attractive angry elf—differently attractive...

Cam knew he should be thinking about the conversation, but he understood only too well what she was saying. He'd scoured the internet for information on battered women the previous evening and everything he'd heard from Jo fitted into what he'd read.

'There are successes, too, of course,' she was saying, pressing her hands to her cheeks as if she knew they'd grown pink. 'And Jackie could be one. I suspect she's made the move now because of the boys. Jared is going on ten, which is an age where he could intervene between his parents and get hurt, or he could begin to ape his father's behaviour and start verbally, or even physically, abusing Aaron.'

'I kind of gathered the second scenario might be happening—and that was just from a fifteen-minute car ride.'

Fine dark eyebrows rose above the green witch eyes.

'Ah!' she said. 'I did wonder. The good thing is, Lauren will get them sorted. There is absolutely no violence allowed in the refuge—no smacking of kids, no kids hitting or punching each other, no verbal abuse or threatening behaviour full stop.'

Cam kind of heard the reply, but his mind had drifted—well, the new door he'd shut was open again and he was wondering what those eyes would look like fired with an emotion other than anger.

Desire perhaps...

He tried to shut the door—this was *not* the time to be fantasising about his boss. Fantasising about any woman, really. He was heading north along the coast, surfing to clear his head, working because that helped as well, trying to come to terms with the fact that the emotional baggage he'd picked up in his army life—the damage from makeshift bombs, the deaths of innocent bystanders, the broken, lost and orphaned children—would probably stay with him for ever, he just had to learn how to deal with it.

As Jackie had to learn to deal with the myriad annoyances of officialdom—

'The fish for you?'

The surfing waiter had returned, sliding a bowl of steaming calamari in front of Jo, then placing Cam's plate on the table in front of him.

'Enjoy!' the young man said, and he bounced away. Cam could feel the excitement the young surfer was trying to keep under control in his body as he looked forward to a future following his dream.

'Was this always your dream?'

Given the way he'd been thinking, it had been a natural question to ask, but from the way Jo was frowning at him, it must have come out wrong.

'Eating calamari in the surf club?' she queried. 'Well, I do enjoy it but it was hardly a lifelong ambition.'

He had to laugh.

'Being a doctor, coming back to work in your home town, working with your father? Was it always your ambition in the way going on the pro tour has been our waiter's ambition? Was it that ambition that kept you off the pro tour?'

She could lie and say yes, kill the conversation once and for all, but his laugh had been so natural, so heartfelt and open and full of fun, she found it difficult to lie to him.

'Not always.' She was going to make do with that when she realised he wasn't going to be satisfied and would ask more questions. 'Any more than surfing your way along the coast was probably yours. Things happen, people change, dreams are reshaped to fit.'

She put down her fork and looked directly at him, although she knew how dangerous that was. The intensity in his eyes, the quirky lips, a faint scar she'd discovered in his left eyebrow—things that combined to start ripples and flickers and twitches and such churning in her stomach she doubted she'd be able to finish her calamari.

'I don't think this is a bad thing. I'm happy with my reshaped life,' she told him, ignoring all the turmoil going on inside her. 'Very happy!'

That should stop him asking any more personal questions, she told herself as she picked up her fork and stirred the remaining strips of pale, translucent seafood.

Cam clamped his teeth together so the questions he wanted to ask wouldn't escape. What *had* her dream been? What had happened for her to change direction—to reshape her life? Her sister's death? More than that?

It was none of his business.

He was moving on.

Okay, so now he'd suggested the men's pro-gramme, he could set it up, but someone else could run it.

He looked out at the ocean, black and mysteri-ous, always moving, changing, reshaping itself and the land it slid onto or crashed against, and all at once he knew he didn't want to move on—didn't want to leave this place—and not entirely because of the good surf.

Or the fact that getting a programme set up and running would be a terrific challenge.

She'd argued, as he guessed she would, over the bill, but he'd insisted on paying, so she'd walked out of the restaurant in front of him, slowing on the steps, allowing him to catch up as she reached the ground.

'Is there a good track up onto the headland?' he asked, thinking a walk would be a pleasant way to end the day.

Actually, thinking he'd like to spend more time in this woman's company, and what better than a walk in the moonlight?

'Yes,' she said, and something in the way she said it—hard, abrupt—stopped him making the suggestion. But before he could decide whether he wanted to argue, she sighed and turned towards the dark shape of the headland.

'Come on, let's do it,' she said. 'I've put it off long enough.'

Cam had no idea what she meant, but he was delighted she would walk with him no matter what her reasoning.

She set a brisk pace, but his strides were so much longer than hers, it made it easy for him to keep up. Low scrubby bushes, wind-bent, leaned across the path, the smell of salt and the moonlight, wrapping them in a secret world. The shushing of the surf onto the beach, occasional cries of night-hunting birds and the ever-present crashing of the waves against the rocks reminded Cam of all the reasons it was good to be alive.

Good to be alive with a pretty woman by his side?

'The problem with loving people is…' the pretty woman announced, in a voice that told him her mood might not have been as upbeat as his. They'd paused about halfway up the track at a fenced lookout that gave a fantastic view along the southern beach and were leaning on the railing.

'The problem,' she repeated, 'is that you have

to give yourself in love—bits of yourself—
diminishing you and making you vulnerable so
that when something happens to the person you
love, it leaves a hole in your soul. You have to
regrow those bits to make yourself whole again,
but I don't know whether you can ever refill that
hole in your soul.'

He understood she wasn't really talking to him,
more giving voice to her thoughts so she could
sort them out. Now she'd been silent so long, leaning on the railing, dark against the light of the
ocean's reflected moonlight, he wondered if he
should prompt her, or maybe simply walk on and
let her catch up.

No, he couldn't do that.

He waited, looking at the beach but always with
her silhouette at one side of his view, so he saw
the moment when she shrugged off whatever mel-
ancholy had gripped her and turned towards him,
a sad half-smile lingering on her face.

'I'm sorry—I didn't know that stuff was waiting
to come out. Talk about needing a counsellor!'

She shrugged again.

'My sister, my twin, was injured off this headland. It had been our playground all our lives,
then suddenly I found I couldn't come here. Even

now, I don't want to go on up to the top. I thought I could, after all this time, but I can't. She didn't die at once, brain-injured, though, a paraplegic for the ten years that she lived after the accident.'

'Oh, Jo!'

Her name slipped from his lips as his arms folded her against him—a comforting embrace for a woman who was obviously still lost in her grief. He knew from the talk of the patients he'd seen that she would do anything for anyone, had seen her care and concern for Jackie, but who supported Jo? The patients' questioning of him, and their not-so-subtle innuendoes had told him she didn't have a man in her life.

Had she cut herself off from others because love had hurt so much?

Was her passion for the refuge a substitute for love?

He tightened his hold on her, aware that she was relaxing against him now, although when first he'd held her, her body had been stiff and awkward.

'You do know a load is easier to carry when there's someone to help you with it, don't you?' he murmured against her tangle of hair.

She stirred then looked up at him, her face lit

by the bright moon, the slightest of smiles playing around her pink lips.

'And just how much of your load are you sharing?' she asked. 'The load you're trying to drown in the surf?'

Had he mentioned his baggage?

Surely not.

So she'd divined it somehow—guessed he'd carry some unresolved mental trauma from his army experience?

Or she *was* a witch!

He'd never kissed a witch.

The thought startled him so much he dropped his arms, and the moonlit face he'd almost kissed disappeared from view.

Jo eased herself out of his arms, bewildered by her reluctance to move. Surely she hadn't mistaken a comforting hug for something more personal?

Although a glint,or maybe a gleam-in his eyes—just then at the end—had made her think he might—

No way! As *if* he'd been about to kiss her...

He must be feeling so uncomfortable, poor man, and wondering if his boss was some kind of lunatic.

Luna—moon—was it moon-madness that she'd blurted out her pain to him?

Made him feel obliged to give her a hug?

The problem was her memories of Jill had come slinking and creeping back into her mind from the moment she'd seen Cam in the flat—the stranger in amongst the roses. Then the talk of surfing and reshaped dreams at dinner, and to top it all off, Cam's suggestion they walk up the headland.

Jo's first instinct had been to say no, but she'd known she had to do it one day. She loved the headland and for one crazy moment she'd thought it might complete her rebuilding—make her whole again—ready to move on...

'To lose a sibling is bad enough, but a twin... No wonder you felt you'd lost pieces of yourself.'

He'd slid an arm around her shoulders and was guiding her back down the path as if the little interlude—the hug and possibly the almost kiss— had never happened. His voice was deep, and gentle, and understanding, and it made her want to cry, which was stupid as she had finished her crying a long time ago.

'Yes,' she finally agreed, hoping he hadn't heard her sniff or swallow the lump that had lodged in her throat, 'but I'm obviously not as back together as I thought I was. I'm sorry to have dumped all that on you. It just came flooding out.'

'Better out than in,' her companion said, and although the remark was beyond trite, Jo knew in this case it was certainly true. She felt a whole lot better—apart from feeling slightly weepy.

They drove home in silence, but as the security lights came on in the carport and Jo knew he'd see the tears she'd been surreptitiously wiping away on the drive, she apologised once again.

'Think nothing of it,' Cam told her. 'Feel free to vent any time. In fact, I should give you fair warning that one day some of my baggage might come tumbling out. You were right in thinking I had stuff to drown during my surf odyssey.'

To Cam's surprise Jo reached over and touched his arm.

'I'm sure that stuff, or baggage as you call it, is far more valid than mine,' she said softly. 'To have seen young men killed and injured in war— to have to mend their bodies and hopefully help heal their minds—I can't imagine the strength it must have taken.'

Cam covered her small hand with his large one, and felt the fragility of her bones beneath the warm skin.

Bird bones.

'I don't think you can rate the baggage we carry around with us,' he told her. 'I think we all have it and we have to deal with it in our own way, day by day, week by week. Then one day it's not as heavy—at least, that's what I'm expecting-hoping—and as I said, maybe sharing it.'

Could he do that? Share the images that flashed before his eyes? Talk about the horror of his nightmares?

The thought startled him so much he gave her fingers a squeeze and climbed out of the vehicle, anxious now to get away, even if his temporary sanctuary was covered in roses and he'd guessed who had used it originally so he felt even more uneasy about staying in the bower.

But what bothered him most was that he'd *mentioned* his baggage. He hadn't talked to anyone about it—not his parents or any of his sisters, not even, really, his ex-fiancée, who had first labelled the mess in his mind.

Yet here he was warning Jo that he might dump some of it on her.

Not that he could.

Could he?

Headlights probed the sky as a vehicle came

up the steep hill. Jo was still standing beside the driver's door, and some instinct to protect, perhaps not her specifically but any smaller, weaker person, made Cam pause as the big car topped the rise and turned towards the house.

A police vehicle, not flashing red and blue lights but its markings made it unmistakeable. Cam felt the sinews tighten in his chest—police, ambulance, fire vehicles, as far as he was concerned, none of them boded good.

Jo watched Mike Fletcher climb out of his big, official vehicle and felt her stomach clench with anxiety. She was vaguely aware that Cam had moved closer to her, and her body's reaction was enough to make her straighten up and stride away from him, crossing the carport to meet Mike.

'Trouble?' she asked, looking at the chunky, handsome man who'd become a good friend in the two years he'd been at the Cove.

'Richard Trent,' he said, and Jo's clench of anxiety tightened.

'Jackie and the kids?' Jo demanded, and Mike put his hand on her shoulder.

'No, they're fine. Sorry to give you a fright, but Richard called in at the station to report them missing.'

'Tonight? Just now?'

Mike nodded, then introduced himself to Cam, who'd closed in on her again.

Protective?

Jo concentrated on what Mike had come to tell her, about Richard Trent and his reaction in calling the police. Why would Richard have acted so swiftly—indoor cricket would have barely finished and surely calling the police would be a last resort?

'Did he check with any friends or family first?' she asked Mike. 'Phone to see if they'd gone there? Not that they have, of course, they're at the refuge—Lauren would have faxed you.'

Mike shook his head.

'I couldn't believe it when I read the fax and I still find it hard to believe. I mean, Richard's the captain of our indoor cricket team and captain of one of the SES crews—that's probably why he came to me, because he knows me—but Richard violent? Had he attacked her tonight?'

'Abuse isn't always violent, and though he might not have hit her before he left he'd waved his cricket bat at her and warned her he'd be home to deal with her later,' Jo told him. 'Something in his tone or maybe in whatever had transpired to anger him convinced Jackie that he meant it. She was terrified when we collected her.'

Realising that this conversation could more easily take place inside her house, she added, 'Come on in,' including Cam in the offer with a glance his way. She offered drinks that no one wanted and they settled down on the deck—the magical sheen of moonlight on the ocean making talk of violence seem unreal.

'So, if he knows they're in the refuge, why are you here, Mike?'

Cam asked the question and Mike frowned as if he was considering not answering—or maybe wondering what right Cam had to be asking it.

Jo stepped in, explaining Cam was coming to work for her and that he'd been with her when she'd driven Jackie to the refuge.

'Staying here, is he?' Mike asked.

'In the flat,' Jo explained, 'but Cam's right, are you worried about Richard's reaction that you came up here? Was it to warn me he was angry about Jackie's leaving? That I might be a target?'

Mike explained that as he'd never suspected Richard might be violent, he'd had no idea what the upset man might do and had thought it best to talk to Jo about it in person.

'Cam's suggested setting up a programme for men with abuse issues,' she said. 'Something that could be ongoing because, as we all know, physical and mental abuse is like substance abuse, it goes in cycles. So although the offender wants desperately to kick the habit, so to speak, it's nearly impossible without strong, ongoing support.'

Cam didn't expect Mike to greet this plan with overwhelming enthusiasm, but a nod of acceptance or a 'Good idea, mate' might have been appropriate. But maybe because he, Cam, was a stranger in town, Mike had a policeman's natural suspicion of him.

Small towns sure were different from the city…

'If you're a friend of Richard's, maybe you could talk to him about it,' Jo continued.

'Hard to do that if he doesn't admit to being abusive,' Mike replied. 'It'd put me in the position of deciding he's guilty whether he is or not, and that would certainly be offensive to him.'

Cam could see Mike's point.

'You don't want to ruin a friendship by stepping in,' Cam told him. 'The man might need help but he needs his friends to stick by him as well. From what I've read, most of the men attending programmes have been ordered to attend by the courts.'

Jo sighed and nodded at him.

'You're right, but less than fifty per cent of our women ever take their partners to court or even get a domestic violence order against them.'

'I can't see that a programme would work if we're expecting men who don't believe they're abusive to attend voluntarily,' Mike told her.

'But we need to get it started. As well as helping men learn to react in non-violent ways, which I accept is the main reason for such a programme, it's just the kind of thing that could add to our worth as far as the funding bodies are concerned. That could help keep the refuge open,' Jo replied. 'It's exactly the kind of thing that they—the relevant government departments—like to see happening. It would fit into their blueprint for long-term solutions for battered women, and it would show we have an integrated service instead of just a safe place for women to stay on a temporary basis.'

'Could we work it through the women's support group that Lauren runs?' Cam suggested, not liking the desperation in Jo's voice and pleased to be able to add something useful to the conversation. 'What if the women concerned could make their partner's attendance in a programme a condition of their returning to the relationship— would that work?'

'It might,' Jo said, offering a rather tired smile— a tired smile that reminded him that it had already been a long day, with more than enough emotion involved, first of all collecting Jackie, then Jo's unhappiness on the walk up the headland.

'It's not the best time to be discussing this,' Cam said firmly. 'We need to get together, maybe get Tom on board as well, and definitely Lauren, and see how we can make a men's programme work.' He turned to Mike. 'Now, do you think Richard Trent represents a danger to Jo? If so, I'm happy to sleep in my camper in the carport. Any vehicle approaching would wake me with its lights.'

Mike looked put out, as if Cam had undermined his official authority somehow.

'I doubt Richard Trent would take his anger out on Jo,' Mike admitted.

'I'll be fine so go home, both of you,' Jo told them. 'We'll talk again tomorrow. Cam's idea of all of us getting together is a good one. I can organise an afternoon with no appointments later in the week—is Friday all right for you, Mike?'

'This week it's okay—next week is schoolies and chaos. But, yes, if you can get Tom and Lauren, we could have it at the community centre in town and brainstorm some ideas.'

Jo led the two men back through the house to the carport, fully expecting Cam to peel off and go into the flat, but, no, he hung around while Mike said goodbye, hung around as Mike drove off, then, as she was beginning to wonder if he'd ever go inside, he touched her lightly on the shoulder.

'Why don't you sleep in the flat—in the second bedroom—just in case?'

They'd been moving enough for the sensor light to have remained on, so she was able to look up into his face, but she could read nothing there but concern and kindness.

'Just in case this man turns up,' he clarified, then, as if aware she could barely fathom the offer, let alone make a decision, he added, 'Go on! You know it's the safest option. I'll wait here while you get your gear and toothbrush, but don't fuss around—I need to get to bed if I'm going to catch a wave before work in the morning.'

Jo went.

It wasn't as if she hadn't spent time in the flat before, she reminded herself. She'd lived there in the rose garden when her father had still been living in the house—when she had been working with him after Jilly's death.

And an angry Richard Trent was an unknown quantity to all of them, so it made sense to sleep in the flat.

In a bedroom right next door to Fraser Cameron?

The same Fraser Cameron who'd held her in his arms, comforted her, and for a moment made her think he might have kissed her?

The same Fraser Cameron who made her stomach drop when she turned and saw him unexpectedly?

Well, she wouldn't be seeing him unexpectedly, would she? She'd be in one bedroom and he'd be in the other and she could stay in bed until he went for a surf then scurry back home to shower and get ready for work.

It would be okay…

And it was.

Right up until she walked into the flat and saw him in the boxer shorts he obviously wore to bed. Not tight enough to be too revealing, they still clung to a butt that could make any woman swoon, while the bare chest, a toasty brown with a scattering of dark hairs, made her knees go weak.

Attraction shouldn't be so strong so quickly. It must be that she was tired and over-emotional that this man's body was tugging at hers, as if invisible threads—finer than spiders' webs—were tangling them together.

'Hot chocolate?'

She heard the words but the picture they conjured up—licking chocolate off that chest, dipping her tongue into a chocolate-filled navel—made her groan out loud.

'You don't like hot chocolate?'

She dragged her eyes upwards to his face and caught an expression of disbelief.

'I thought everyone liked hot chocolate,' he added, with such a warm, open smile she felt doubly ashamed of her thoughts and could feel blood rushing to her cheeks to make her shame obvious.

'Not tonight,' she managed in a garbled voice, and she fled to the second bedroom, so pleased to escape him she had to open the door she'd shut behind her to call out a goodnight.

After which she shut it firmly once again and collapsed onto the bed.

What was happening to her?

Easy to answer that. She was falling in lust with her employee.

And just where would that get her?

Given that he was the epitome of tall, fairly dark and extremely handsome and could obviously have any woman he wanted and wouldn't look twice at a scrawny redhead, absolutely nowhere, that's where.

Not that she wanted this inexplicable attraction to go anywhere. Love led to loss in her experience and she wasn't ready to lose any more bits of herself.

Love? Where had love come into the equation? She'd been thinking lust—nothing more.

CHAPTER SIX

THE flat was curiously empty when she awoke, feeling surprisingly refreshed, the next morning. Her tenant's bedroom door was open, revealing the rose-covered spread drawn tightly across the bed—army training no doubt—but it was in the kitchen, where she went to get a glass of water, that the surprise awaited her. A plate of fruit, but set out like a smiley face, two cherries for the eyes, a slice of pawpaw for a nose, a curved banana for a mouth. Balls of orange rockmelon curled around the face, while her name was spelled out in carefully cut pieces of watermelon—a riot of colour, taste and nutrition.

Assuming he didn't make himself smiley-face fruit breakfasts every morning, it meant he'd done it especially for her.

Wanting to get in good with her so he could stay on permanently?

Or simply because he was a kind and thoughtful man?

A little pang inside her suggested that she'd like to think it was because he liked her, maybe was a little bit attracted to her, but common sense prevailed and she took the plate through to her house, apparently undisturbed overnight, and ate the fruit as she got ready for work.

Work.

She had to contact the Bennetts to find out if they'd decided what they wanted to do about a sleep programme for Kaylin, talk to Cam about IVF and Helene, contact Tom and Lauren to see if Friday afternoon suited them for a meeting...

She'd walked onto the deck as she was finishing the fruit and considering the day ahead, and now she sighed, thinking of Cam out there on his board, wishing for the first time in years that she was out there too.

Which reminded her of Cam's promise to young Aaron. She was pretty sure the baby boards on which she and Jill had learnt to surf were in the storeroom downstairs. She'd check on her way down to work. They'd be ideal for the two little boys, though Cam couldn't handle both of them safely on his own. Would Jackie join in surfing lessons?

Now it was a squirmy kind of disturbance in

Jo's stomach. No, she wouldn't help. Bad enough having to work with a man to whom her body was attracted, but out of office hours?

At the beach?

No way.

Never!

'Can I help?'

The offer startled her as she was hauling the boards out from behind other cast-off rubbish in the storeroom beneath the deck, sorry she hadn't left the task until after work, because her hands were filthy and she was covered with dust.

Her tenant, standing in the doorway, was also ready for work—but clean.

'Thanks, but I've found what I was looking for,' she told him, not that he appeared the slightest bit interested in her reply, for he was lifting her old board—the last board she'd had specially shaped to her own design before she'd stopped surfing—running his hands over its smooth lines, the delight on his face suggesting he'd just discovered hidden treasure.

'It's a Silver Crowne,' he said, in awed tones. 'I've heard of these boards but never seen one up close. Silver Crowne only made pro boards.'

The slight accusation in the final sentence made Jo stiffen, but she refused to answer him, passing him the small boards instead.

'Mind your clothes, these are still dusty,' she said, 'although most of the dust seems to have transferred itself to me. I thought they might do for the Trent boys.'

Cam grinned at her.

'Wow, great idea. Teaching them to surf is a far better idea than taking them for one ride on my board. You'll help?'

No was the obvious answer, but somehow it failed to come out. Jo made a big deal of dusting off her clothes, then gave up.

'I'll just run upstairs, have a quick shower and change into something clean—tell Kate I'll be down in a few minutes.'

He seemed to accept she wasn't going to reply for he asked, 'Will these boards be safe if we leave them out, or should we lock them back in your storeroom but near the front?'

Jo was halfway out the door when she realised he was still holding the boards—*and* she hadn't thanked him for breakfast.

'We'll leave them just inside and if you could shut the door and close the padlock that would be great. And thank you for the breakfast, it made my morning.'

She looked into the blue eyes she'd been avoiding since he'd appeared in the storeroom and read kindness in them, nothing more, she was sure, yet her heart was skipping around like a wayward wallaby, and some stupid sector of her brain was whispering it might be more than lust.

Which was impossible.

Lust at first sight was possible—she had no doubts about that—but anything else?

She wasn't going to give the alternative 'L' word brain space.

Cam watched her dash away. She'd coloured as she'd thanked him for the breakfast that some fit of hitherto undiscovered whimsy had prompted him to make for her. Had he embarrassed her?

He didn't have a clue. For some reason, all the useful information on how women thought, stuff his brain had collected from his sisters and his ex-fiancée, was no help at all in figuring out this particular woman.

Though why he thought it should when he'd only known her, what—less than two days.

And why it mattered…

He pondered these things as he made his way

down the steps to the surgery, deciding in the end that it was because his body was attracted to her that his brain was confused.

Well, it would just have to stay confused, because he wasn't going to act on the attraction. Honour was important in the army and how honourable would he be if he did act on the attraction? How could he have an affair with a woman when he was still getting over his experiences in the war, still getting vivid flashes of injured and dying young men, still hearing echoes of their cries in his ears, and not only when he was asleep?

He knew these flashbacks sent him into a kind of shock, making him withdraw, making him appear all the things Penny had said he was—remote, detached, morose—cutting him off from whatever company he was in.

Could he land some other woman with those mood swings?

Make her suffer as Penny must have to have broken off the engagement?

Best to stay unattached.

Jo heaved a sigh of relief when she saw Kate and one of the nurses in the lunch-room. No need for one-on-one again with Dr Cameron, although Cam wasn't present and, no, she wasn't going to wonder where he was. He could have been delayed with a patient, or gone shopping, surfing, anything.

Avoiding her as she would like to be avoiding him?

Her relief was short-lived.

'Heard you and the new doc in town, our delectable Dr Cam, were dining together at the surf club last night,' Kate said brightly, and too late Jo remembered Kate's brother was the apprentice chef at the club.

Small towns.

'We were eating together—late. It had been a long day.' Jo hoped her repressive tone would stop further conversation, but she'd bargained without Kate's persistence.

'Moonlight on the water, was there?'

'Where? When?' Cam *would* choose that moment to come into the room. Not that he seemed interested in the answer, already delving into the refrigerator to check out the sandwiches on offer today.

'Last night,' Kate told him. 'The view from the surf club. Romantic?'

Cam looked up at her and grinned.

'Now I know what your boss means when she talks about small towns.' He put enough emphasis on the 'your' to make Kate look a little uncomfortable. 'For your information, we'd just completed an errand of mercy, it was late, and we were hungry. It was the surf club or fast food.'

He turned to look at Jo.

'Was the moon out? Can you remember?'

Jo was so pleased he'd diverted the conversation she smiled at him.

'Far too interested in my calamari to notice,' she said, then she turned to Ellie, the nurse who did shifts at the surgery and the hospital, to ask about the babies' sleep programme.

But she was aware that the community interest she'd foretold when she'd taken Cam on board was already rife, and with a small twinge of sadness accepted there'd be no more dinners at the surf club with him.

Or was she being silly?

She could handle talk, especially talk that had no basis in fact.

Although given the instant lust thing going on, there was probably a teeny, tiny basis...

'Are you listening?' Ellie demanded.

'Of course,' Jo told her, hoping her mind could rerun Ellie's explanation for her. 'You need at least four nights. If we could get Amy in over a weekend—starting Friday and running through to Tuesday—it might be easier for Todd to get help with the milking.'

'If you left it until the school holidays—another couple of weeks—there might be a high school kid who'd be happy to have the work.'

Obviously Cam had been following the conversation better than she had, that he'd come up with such a sensible suggestion, although—

'If Kaylin's sleep avoidance is as bad as Amy suggested, another couple of weeks might be too long to wait,' Jo told him.

'What about an in-home arrangement?' Coming from Cam, this second suggestion was so surprising Jo had to ask.

'You've been in the army, not general practice, what would you know about in-home arrangements?'

He gave her a smug smile—but even smug it tickled her sensitive bits.

'Three sisters and at last count eight nieces and nephews. One of my sisters had terrible trouble with her second baby and she got someone to come in.'

He turned to Ellie.

'It sounds as if you're involved in the programme at the hospital. What exactly do you do?'

Ellie straightened in her chair and Jo realised she wasn't the only one in the practice who was feeling the effect of the pheromones that had infiltrated the atmosphere with Cam's arrival.

'We put the mum to bed in a separate room and one nurse stays up with the baby, handling it when it wakes. We don't use controlled crying, but use a coaching technique that we've found successful. It's best with babies who've started solids three times a day, and usually it works in three nights, though we say four in case we need the extra night.'

Jo thought about it then nodded.

'Kaylin's six months old and she's on solids. In fact, although she's still being breastfed, I suggested Amy try her on them when she came in about sleep problems earlier.'

She was still thinking about Kaylin when Cam entered the conversation again.

'If you're doing this programme at the hospital, would you be willing to do it at their home?'

Cam realised he'd gone too far—taken the extra step when it was Jo who should be making decisions about her staff deployment.

He turned to her, hands up in the air.

'Sorry, I shouldn't be making suggestions without consulting you, Jo. You're Ellie's employer, not me, but I get carried away.'

Fortunately Jo wasn't put out, flashing him a cheeky smile before saying, 'I was wondering when you'd remember that, but it's an excellent idea. Ellie, if you'd be happy to do it, I'd be happy to pay you for the four nights—and days so you can sleep. What are your hospital shifts like? Could you fit it in some time soon?'

'Next week,' Ellie told her. 'I'd love to give it a go. I don't have hospital shifts next week because I refuse to work schoolies week. Tom gets contract nurses in, and I'm off duty here as well.'

Cam felt a surge of satisfaction out of all proportion to the small contribution he'd made—a surge that made him think maybe general practice in a smallish town would have a lot of rewards, and in this town he'd have the added attraction of fantastic surf.

If he could persuade Jo to let him stay.

Hmm, maybe not such a good idea, given how

aware he was of her. Even sitting in a lunch-room with two other women, his body was conscious of every move Jo made, his mind considering changes in the inflections of her voice. Last night, knowing she was sleeping the other side of a fairly flimsy wall, he'd imagined things an employee should never imagine about his boss, no matter how attractive he found her.

Sleep had eluded him for hours, although that was probably just as well, given the aforementioned flimsy wall. He would have hated to have awakened her with his nightmares.

He tuned back into the conversation in time to hear Jo asking Ellie to phone Amy to make the arrangements, then, as Ellie and Kate left the room, he turned to the woman who'd so disturbed *his* sleep.

'Can you afford to be paying Ellie to do the sleep programme? Will you charge the parents of the baby? Are such things covered by government subsidies?'

She turned towards and smiled—second smile in one lunch-break, not that he was counting.

'Worried I won't be able to afford your salary?' she teased, then the smile slid off her face as she added, 'I'm sure there are government subsidies, if I wanted to research them and then do the paperwork, but I can afford to pay Ellie for her time. If this works, we can find out about possible subsidies for the future, but for now, if we can provide four good nights' sleep for Amy and Todd, I'm happy to cop the cost. If it succeeds, well, it's worth more than money to the Bennetts.'

'Four uninterrupted nights' sleep,' Cam said, wondering if he'd ever reach that blissful pinnacle himself. And thinking of that goal, he was less guarded than he usually was. 'Are there sleep programmes for grown-ups as well as kids?'

She looked startled at first, his boss, then he read such compassion in her eyes he knew if he wasn't very careful, he could easily drown in those green depths.

'I wondered that myself after my sister died,' she said softly, then offered him a third smile, and though it lacked the spark of the earlier smiles, it affected him more deeply than either of the earlier ones had.

She rested her hand on his arm.

'For me, it did get easier in time and I'm sure it will for you. Are they nightmares you suffer? Dreams so vivid and horrific you really don't want to sleep?'

She didn't wait for a reply, simply tightening her fingers on his arm as she added, 'That cliché about time being a great healer isn't just a trite expression—we know that in our work.'

Cam looked down at the small hand, pale against his tanned skin, and felt an urge to hold it for ever—to let it haul him out of where he'd been and into hope and life and...

Love?

Surely not.

They'd finished seeing patients by five in the afternoon, making Jo remember the time when she'd worked with her father, the pair of them taking turns to have free afternoons, he to sail with Molly, his new-found love, while she had worked with Lauren on plans for the refuge.

'So, surfing lessons for the little boys?' Cam suggested as they left the surgery.

Jo considered protesting but with daylight saving they had three full hours before sunset, and the sun still held enough heat to make the thought of hitting the surf very attractive.

Not that she'd surf, just help the boys as they tried the boards in the water—teach them how to balance on the boards.

'I'll phone the refuge and speak to Jackie,' she told Cam as he strode up the steps beside her. 'The key to the storeroom padlock is—'

'Above the door?' he guessed, and she felt her face heat.

'I know it's stupid—I'll stop doing it. It's just that growing up here, no one locked their doors and if you drove down the road for a bottle of milk, you usually left your keys in the car while you popped into the shop. Small towns were safe places.'

'For everyone?'

She knew exactly what he meant. Violence against women in some form or another had probably been around for ever.

'Probably not, although I wonder if the more hectic pace of life that we lead now and the expectations we put on ourselves might not have made abuse within relationships more prevalent.'

'Who knows? But it would be interesting to find if there's documented history of it anywhere.'

Jo smiled, suddenly seeing a different side of the man who'd come to work for her, a side not unlike a side of herself—the bit that always wanted to know more, to delve deeper.

'I think I'll concentrate on the now—on keeping the refuge open—and leave the history for my retirement.'

His reply was one of his quirky smiles, lighting up his face, easing the strain that lined it in repose.

'I'll change and get the boards,' he told her. 'Say half an hour? Will we need to collect the boys or will someone drive them to the beach?'

'I'll get them—well, we'll get them—silly to take two cars. I can put the boards, your board as well, on the top of my car. I think the southern beach will be the best this afternoon. It will be less crowded and there should be some white wash close to the shore. That's best for beginners.'

Cam's smile widened, but this time it wasn't anything to do with their previous conversation— more to do with his passion for riding the waves.

'Great—I haven't surfed there yet.'

'You're going there to teach the boys,' Jo reminded him, although when she'd seen the smile and heard the passion in his voice she'd felt a pang of longing.

'I'll have to show them, too,' he reminded her, before turning to unlock the storeroom and retrieve the small boards.

* * *

How had he inveigled her into this? Jo wondered as she drove Cam and two excited little boys down the track onto the southern beach, then along it on the hard sand near the water, looking for a spot that would be good for the lessons?

'Do I need a permit to drive my van along here?' Cam asked. 'I checked out the beach near the headland, where it's accessible, and saw vehicles driving south, but didn't know if anyone could do it.'

'You need a permit but they're easy to get. You can apply at the local council office.'

She pulled up where a lagoon had formed close to the beach, the surf breaking on a sand bank further out. The little boys tumbled out of the vehicle, their faces white with sun-screen, rash shirts covering their chests, arguing over who got what board the moment Cam lifted them down onto the sand.

'We start on the beach,' Jo told them. 'Board on the sand, then lie on it, rise up to kneel on it, then stand and balance on it. The fin will make it a bit wobbly but not nearly as wobbly as it will seem on the water. Left foot in front, right foot behind unless you're goofy footers—'

Both boys laughed, pointing at each other and

calling each other goofy footers while Jo explained the term for surfers who put their right foot forward.

'Now, feet in place, knees bent to keep you balanced, arms held out like this.'

'Here,' Cam said, dropping his board in front of her, 'if you're being Teach, you should show them.'

He was so close—his nose, too, white with cream, his chest, at the moment, modestly covered with a tattered T-shirt, but so big, so male!—she felt a shiver of pure, yes, lust run through her. But could lust be classified as pure?

She stood on his board, demonstrating the stance, thinking that if she'd brought her board she could have used it on the sand and Cam could have surfed—well away from her. But the image of the water droplets on his chest came vividly back into her head.

Just as well he wasn't surfing…

'This is too easy!' Jared's complaint brought her back to earth.

'Okay, we'll try it in the water, and for this first lesson you probably won't be standing up. We'll be in the shallows, showing you how to catch the wave.'

Jared began to argue, silenced only when Jo pointed out that there was no point learning to stand up on a board if you couldn't paddle to catch the wave in the first place.

She bent to lift Aaron's board, but Cam stopped her.

'Nothing doing,' he said. 'Surfers always carry their own boards, don't they, boys?'

He showed them how to tuck the boards under their arms, holding them about midway to balance them, then, a little boy on either side of him, the tall man headed for the water.

Thankfully still with his broad chest decently covered.

Jo slipped off the long T-shirt she'd pulled on over her bikini, hoping she wasn't wiping off all the sunscreen she'd slathered on her pale body.

She was feeling a squirmy kind of embarrassment at appearing so skimpily dressed in front of a virtual stranger, and an employee at that, but it was far too hot to wear a wetsuit, so her bikini had been her only option.

Exactly as he'd pictured her—the curvy body, and pale, pale skin—Cam's heart skipped a beat then Jared butted him with his surfboard, prob-

NEW DOC IN TOWN

ably accidentally but definitely bringing Cam's attention back to the surfing lesson.

'I'll hold your board, and Dr Jo will hold Aaron's,' he said. 'When you're actually surfing, you don't stand around on your board, you sit on it, waiting for a wave, legs dangling over the side, then you lie on it to paddle onto the wave, so we'll start sitting then lying down paddling to catch a wave. Once you've done that a few times, you can try standing up, but usually that's in your second lesson.'

Jared, of course, wanted to stand immediately and fell off innumerable times before he agreed that maybe paddling to catch waves was fun as well. Jo's pupil was more wary, perhaps a little scared, but he had plenty of determination, working his little arms furiously through the water as he paddled to put his board into the white wash of the waves.

'Enough lessons for one day,' Jo eventually said to the boys as the sun dipped low enough to throw shadows from the dunes across the beach. She turned to Cam. 'Why don't you catch a few waves while I run the boys back to their mother and have a chat to Lauren about the meeting? I'll drive back and collect you in an hour.'

'You don't have to do that. I can go home and get the van.'

'But you can't drive down the beach without a permit,' she reminded him.

Beyond the lagoon, the surf was so tempting Cam gave in, paddling out through the breakers to the calm beyond them, aware that at this time in his life he was more at peace out here on the ocean than anywhere else in the world. Out here the world was forgotten, his only thought which of the set of waves coming towards him would provide the best ride.

Except that today peace, as he'd come to know it, eluded him. He was studying the sets, as usual, picking out the likely waves, but images of Jo kept intruding so he missed the first wave he'd picked out, no amount of paddling enabling him to catch it.

He caught the next one, paddled back out, but after missing another curling green beauty he gave up, sat on his board, legs dangling, and thought about distractions. His psychology studies had taught him that humans are programmed for flight or fight. Adrenalin would pump into the body to help either option. Instinct told us to look out for danger, to predict it and in so doing work out how to avoid it.

Wouldn't that work with emotions as well as physical situations? He knew the attraction he felt towards Jo represented danger—not physical danger but it put at risk his immediate plan, which was to get his head sorted. And having predicted the danger, shouldn't he avoid it—get away from the woman who was distracting him so much?

For her sake more than his!

Yes, he should flee.

And leave her without a second doctor at the busiest time of her year? Very valiant that would be!

CHAPTER SEVEN

WITH an effort, Cam pushed these thoughts behind the new door, the one now labelled 'Jo', and concentrated on the surf, although his concentration was lost again when she returned, pulling up on the beach. She reached into the back of her vehicle, and took out the classic old surfboard he'd admired earlier.

She was buffeted by the waves as she paddled her way out beyond the breakers, and it was obvious that it had been a while since she'd surfed, but when she came alongside him and he saw the sheer joy lighting her face, he stopped worrying about her. Even if the lad at the surf-club restaurant hadn't mentioned she'd been good, he'd have guessed. It was evident in the way she lay on the board, the effortless way she paddled, and now, as she sat, the long-distance focus in her eyes as she stared out to sea made her experience obvious.

'I'm taking the fifth wave in this set and if you

drop in on me I'll probably kill you. It's been thirteen years since I've been on a board, and that's *my* wave!'

She paddled sideways towards it, rising into a crouch as the wave caught the board then standing up but still tilted forward so her body mimicked the curve of the wave as she slashed across its face. She bent into the barrel, flying out the other end, her cry one of delight but of triumph as well.

She rode the board towards the beach, standing upright now, as if she owned the ocean, sliding right onto the sandbank. Then, to Cam's surprise, and just a little dismay, she pushed her board into the lagoon, paddled across it, then picked it up and returned it to her vehicle.

He caught the next wave and rode it well enough, but without a thousandth of the grace and skill he'd just witnessed. Assuming she wanted to go home, he, too, paddled across the lagoon, then tucked his board under his arm and strode up the beach to where she waited, wrapped in a towel, still flushed with the excitement she must have felt as she'd ridden a perfect ten.

'Thirteen years?' he queried as he fastened his

board next to the small ones on the racks on top of the car.

He regretted the words almost immediately as the excitement died from her eyes and the flush faded from her cheeks.

'Let's go home,' she said, not the words but the way she said them telling him to keep his questions to himself.

And hadn't he just decided that's what he should do?

Predict and avoid emotional danger, remember. In all fairness he had to stay but he had to build a wall between himself and his boss—invisible but no less strong for that—a wall that would keep his emotions at bay, and if it didn't stop the attraction he felt towards her, well, that was too bad.

He climbed into the car beside her.

She shouldn't have done it! The words hammered in Jo's head.

But for those few minutes she'd felt truly alive again. Was that so wrong?

Of course it was, when Jill was dead.

She closed her eyes against the tears welling in them.

Surely she'd shed enough by now. Bad enough

it had taken a year to draw a pain-free breath, but to still be crying for Jilly?

'You okay?'

Cam's voice reminded her that this was the last person to whom she should be showing weakness. He'd probably had natural empathy before he'd studied psychology, so he'd suss out her misery far more quickly than the average person.

She nodded.

'Always drive the beach with your eyes shut, then?' he asked, and the provoking question angered her enough to chase away her maudlin mood.

'I could drive through the whole town with my eyes closed,' she snapped.

'Snippy, eh?' he teased.

'I won't dignify that with an answer,' she said, aiming for snooty but not quite making it, because once again she found a little bit of herself enjoying a bout of verbal sparring with this man.

'But you did,' he pointed out and she sighed, and smiled, steering the big vehicle carefully up over the dune and onto the road.

She put her foot on the brake and turned towards him.

'You win,' she said, then was sorry she'd turned,

for he was smiling at her again, not the quirky smile this time but one in which she could read understanding and, yes, the empathy she'd guessed at.

'Your sister?'

He asked the question—well, said the two words—so quietly, she knew she could ignore them if she wanted to, but deep down she knew it might help to talk about it.

Another sigh.

'You'll hear about it soon enough—someone in town will tell you. Yes, my sister was injured in a surfing accident. When the waves were big we'd get a friend with a powerful jet ski to tow us out beyond the breakers. Jill was being towed out when the rope broke and she was caught by a wave and flung onto the rocks beneath the headland.'

Jo hesitated then found she needed to tell him more.

'What the town doesn't know is that it was my fault. I was the one who wanted to surf that day, although the tail end of the cyclone further north had produced waves far bigger than Jilly liked to tackle. Surfing was *my* passion—the pro tour my ambition.'

The words died on her lips, fading into the silence that filled the vehicle.

'And you gave up your dream? Because you felt guilty?'

The question shocked Jo so much that at first it didn't make sense, then she realised the track his thoughts had taken.

'But I didn't give up my dream—not in a, well, now-I-can't-be-a-pro-surfer kind of way. All I wanted to do was be with her—there was no time for surfing,' she told him. 'Then, because she was so badly injured, because she spent so long in hospitals and rehab centres, and I spent so much time with her, studying medicine seemed a natural thing to do.'

She stared out to sea, replaying her answer in her head then adding, 'I think,' in such a worried, pathetic voice that Cam couldn't help himself.

He reached out and put his arm around her shoulders, shifting so when he drew her closer her head could rest against his chest.

'Sometimes stuff we have shoved into the deep recesses of our minds needs dredging out,' he said quietly, and felt her head nod against his body. Then his other arm snaked around her, and he held her close, dropping a kiss onto the wet red snarls of hair on the top of her head.

'Salty,' he mused then he sniffed, 'and you smell like the sea. It's a good smell, healthy, you should get your hair ocean wet again before too long.'

He was talking to calm her, to reassure her. There was nothing beyond comfort in the hug he was giving her, and if his body didn't agree with that, then too bad.

The warmth of his body crept into Jo's cold one, right into the frozen places that even hot summer weather had failed to warm since Jilly's death. The inner warmth whispered danger, but it whispered—no, shouted—other things as well. Things like desire…

Far harder to handle, desire, than lust. Lust could be put down as a base animal instinct but desire—well, surely that was about softer feelings.

She pushed away from the warmth, and her thoughts.

'Thanks for the hug,' she said, in as matter-of-fact voice as she could summon up. 'I needed it. I didn't realise just how much emotion would come dredging up—to use your words—on the back of one wave. But that's twice I've dredged stuff up to you—now it's your turn.'

He looked startled, but she wasn't relenting.

'Is it just your memories from the army or more than that you're escaping?'

'Escaping?' he echoed, and she had to laugh.

'Of course you're escaping—surfing your way along the coast. Not that it isn't a good way to escape, but can you do it for ever?'

Cam stared at her.

Okay, he was attracted to her, and there was an element of danger in that attraction, but this—this questioning, that was different, disturbing.

'Probably not,' he admitted, and she laughed again.

'That's not nearly enough,' she insisted, touching him on the arm, something she had done before—something he enjoyed her doing. 'I can understand there are probably things you can't talk about—things people who haven't experienced being a doctor in a war zone could never imagine—but you must have known you'd come out of the army one day and had maybe not a dream but an idea of what you wanted to do. Just as Jilly's death changed my career path, was it just the army experience that changed yours?'

It isn't her business, one part of him insisted.

She's impertinent for asking, it added.

But deep inside a longing to share just a little of his turmoil was growing stronger and stronger, and as he looked into her eyes and saw the depth of compassion and understanding there, he knew that this was a woman he could tell.

'I came home remote, detached, even morose—or so my ex-fiancée told me. The psychologist I saw—they run us all past one of them from time to time—dismissed PTSD but pointed out I was pretty close to suffering it, with flashbacks and nightmares. He suggested drugs but surfing is my drug of choice, hence the coastal odyssey.'

He blurted out the words then heard their echo in his head and realised how ridiculous they sounded.

He shouldn't have mentioned the morose part!

How pathetic.

Heaven help him.

'I'd have been way beyond morose.'

How had she picked up on the one thing he regretted? he thought, then tuned back in to what Jo was saying.

'Though I can't imagine anyone the description fits less than you. As for remote and detached—

well, sometimes those are places we all need to be at times.' She squeezed his arm with her slender fingers, sending an electric arc of desire fizzing through his body.

Talk about inappropriate.

He covered her hand with his, hoping, really, to stop the reaction, but touching her while she was touching him seemed to make it worse—far worse.

'And what about this ex-fiancée? Did she dump you because you were remote?'

The zinging in his body was so extreme it took him a moment to compute Jo's words and when he did, and heard the sympathy behind the question, he had to smile.

'Not really,' he told Jo. 'It was more a mutual thing. We'd grown apart even before I went away. Our lives diverged.'

He was about to add that it wasn't a broken heart he was escaping but the gentle tightening of her hand on his arm was so pleasurable he decided to accept a little extra sympathy.

Pathetic, that's what he was…

'Perhaps we should go home,' he finally managed, then immediately regretted it when her hand slid from beneath his and she started the car.

Squinting against the setting sun, Jo turned the car for home, her heart thudding in her chest as she considered how easy it would be to fall if not in love with this man then certainly into bed with him.

No, surely the surge of sympathy she'd felt when he'd mentioned his ex-fiancée was more than lust?

Attraction, would that do?

She should be asking more about the ex-fiancée—or maybe not. Maybe he'd said all he intended saying...

The silence stretched while her mind tossed questions back and forth—how bad had it been in the army? Was the engagement over or did the ex still love the morose man? Cam morose? Not that she, Jo, had seen.

'Have you been on your own since your father left? No wild affairs, no men passing through your life, no blighted romance?'

Jo found the questions so unexpected—and hadn't it been her turn to be probing?—that she had to stop the car again.

'And you're asking because?' she asked, while just a little twinge of hope twittered in her heart.

He raised his eyebrows as if her demand had

surprised him. Then he smiled and she wished she'd just kept driving.

'I just wondered,' he said, oh, so gently, 'whether you might have been punishing yourself for your sister's accident for way too long—not surfing, which you obviously love—and maybe standing back from any kind of close relationship because she can't have one.'

'I suppose I asked for that,' she admitted ruefully, 'telling the story of my life to a psychologist.'

She shifted so she was leaning back against the door, almost out of touching distance—not wanting to touch, although it was so tempting.

Concentrate on the conversation, she told herself. Maybe get *him* talking.

She didn't want to consider why that seemed important right now, so she didn't.

'Do you do it to yourself?' she asked instead. 'Discuss the pros and cons of your surfing escape inside your head? Is it easier to understand grief and loss and horror if you can rationalise it through stuff you've learned from books?'

He smiled again and she *knew* she shouldn't have stopped the car—should have driven straight home and escaped into the house. The problem was, the more she was with this man, the more she wanted to know of him—*and* be with him.

But for all he made noises about maybe staying longer in Crystal Cove, she knew he'd eventually move on.

'I'm not sure it works, doing it to yourself—well, it hasn't so far for me, although every day things look a little brighter and going on gets a little easier,' he said. And this time it was he who touched—reaching out to rest his hand on her arm as she had rested hers on his.

The brush of his fingers on her skin zapped her nerve endings to life and she found herself shivering—not with cold but with a weird mix of excitement and delight.

She definitely shouldn't have stopped the car.

And, no, she wasn't going to cover his hand with hers, as he'd done earlier. Definitely not, although her hand was moving in that direction.

The jangling tones of her mobile stopped the strangeness going on in the car right then and there. She answered it, and listened, her heart sinking in her chest.

'Do you want us to come over?' she asked.

'It's Jackie's choice,' Lauren told her.

Jo closed the phone, not even bothering with

a goodbye, then bumped her forehead gently on the steering-wheel as frustration threatened to overwhelm her.

'Jackie going back to Richard?' Cam asked, his voice deep with concern and understanding.

'Apparently he came to see her when the boys were out with us. He took her for a drive so they could talk. He's just collected all three of them.'

'Surely she'll be safe for a while,' Cam said, and Jo shrugged.

'It's so hard to predict. Yes, I'd say in most cases where a woman goes back, the man does try to control his temper for a while, and in Jackie's case the abuse was more emotional than physical, but Richard's such an unknown quantity, and though Jackie is an intelligent woman, she's lived under his domination for so long now, I wonder if she'll ever be able to break free.'

'Are you *his* doctor?'

Jo looked at Cam, wondering where this was going.

'Richard's? No way. He's one of those men who'd drive three hours down the road rather than trust a woman doctor. He used to see Dad but, then, young men like him rarely see a doctor anyway. He was good at all sports so any injuries he had were mostly sport related. He might see Tom at the hospital now, if he has a strain or sprain.'

She hesitated, wondering why Cam had asked, trying to fathom his thinking.

'Why?' she finally asked.

'I was thinking if he did use the clinic, you could have switched him to me. I couldn't have brought up the subject of abuse, not in any way, but he might be harbouring a grudge against you.'

Jo smiled.

'That's a lovely offer, but I'm a big girl. I can handle myself.'

He shook his head.

'Not so big,' he said, 'and you of all people should know that no one could handle an angry man with a cricket bat.'

The thought of Jackie returning to that situation filled Jo with fear, although the bat, as far as she knew, had been no more than a threat.

'Best we get home,' she said, sliding the vehicle back into gear.

Richard Trent came at ten. Cam couldn't say for certain he'd known the man would come, but his gut feeling—and his knowledge of men from his time in the army—had made him ultra-cautious, so he was sitting not on his deck but in the darkened living room of the flat, music playing softly as he explored the world of programmes for abusive men on his laptop. The backlight of the screen was sufficient for him to read the information offered by the internet.

The vehicle pulled up, a dual-cab, four-wheel-drive ute, a muscle car. At first Cam thought it might be Mike, maybe returning for a private visit to Jo, but as the man came into range of the sensor lights, Cam realised he didn't know him.

Neither did he know Richard Trent, and Jo hadn't answered about having men—or even a man—in her life, so it could be perfectly innocent, but Cam was already out the door, mooching towards his van, the bundle of clean beach towels he'd prepared earlier tucked under his arm.

'Hi!' he said, all innocence. 'Visiting Jo, are you? I'm Fraser Cameron, her new tenant in the flat. Working for her over the holidays.'

The stranger, his face pink but his lips thinned to a white line of anger, stopped about a yard in front of Cam, glaring at him.

'So you're the bastard, are you? Call you Cam, don't they? Cam this, Cam that, my boys haven't stopped, but let me tell you this, Fraser Cameron, *my* name is Richard Trent and you stay away from my kids. If they want to learn to surf, *I'll* teach them, understand?'

Cam held out his free hand in a 'hey, man' gesture, then actually used the words.

'Hey, man, no worries. It was just that Jo found the old boards in her storeroom and, knowing the boys, she thought they might like to try them.'

'Well, they don't and they won't and you can tell that to *Dr* Harris as well. She, of all people, should know how dangerous it is to surf, seeing what it did to her sister.'

It flicked through Cam's mind that Jo had been right—it had taken all of two days for someone to tell him about her sister.

'And tell her to stay away from my wife while you're at it. My family is none of her business, understand?'

Cam nodded, but his mind was whirring. Richard Trent was wound so tightly he was going to unravel totally before too long. Cam had seen it in young soldiers, particularly among those handling new responsibilities, and he knew it was impossible to predict just how the unravelling would happen. It could be an explosive burst, or

a crumble into desperation that could often pre-
cipitate worse results than the explosion.

Could he help Richard Trent unwind in some
way? Offer something to help the man relax? The
fact that Richard hadn't walked away when he'd
finished his warning suggested he might be looking for help, if only subconsciously.

'Have you surfed yourself?' Cam asked.

'Everyone in the Cove surfs,' the man growled,
edging towards his ute. 'I know the boys'll want
to do it some time, but they're better off concentrating on their cricket right now.'

'It's years since I played cricket,' Cam told
him, hoping to keep a conversation going long
enough for Richard to calm down before he got
back behind the wheel of his vehicle. 'Though I
did quite well at it when I was at school. Is there
a local club? I'm probably not staying on at the
Cove—two months' trial run over the holidays—
but if I stayed I'd be interested.'

In a game that would keep me out of the surf
all summer? Cam's head protested, but he could
feel a little of the tension easing out of Richard.

'We're always looking for new members and
we've an indoor cricket comp as well.'

He turned to Cam now, leaning against his ute,

ready to talk a little more, Cam suspected, but rubbing at his left shoulder at the same time.

'You a leftie?' Cam asked. 'A bowler?'

Richard frowned but his voice as he asked, 'How'd you guess?' was less tight.

'Looks like you've got a bit of tendonitis. We've got an ultrasound machine down at the clinic that sometimes helps, and if you wanted to come in some time, I could use it on that shoulder and maybe do a bit of joint manipulation.'

Cam held his breath. He could feel Richard's suspicion coming in waves off his body, yet his shoulder must be very sore for it to be distracting him in this situation.

Was the injury exacerbating the home situation? Was he in so much pain he was taking it out on Jackie?'

Wishing he had more practical experience at dealing with domestic violence situations, Cam remained silent, then was delighted when Richard said, a little grudgingly, 'Could I get an appointment tomorrow?'

'Of course—in fact, if it suits you to come in early, we could make it eight-thirty. I don't officially start until nine, so I could spend some time with you.'

Richard nodded as if agreeing, but through sheer bad luck Jo emerged from the house, a bag of rubbish in her hand, apparently heading for the bin but probably carrying it as an excuse as he, Cam, had carried the towels.

'You!' Richard yelled at her, swinging towards Jo, his hands forming fists, although they hung on arms held rigidly to his sides.

'Keep away from my wife and my kids!'

He flung himself into his car.

'I almost wish he'd slammed the car door,' Cam said as the ute backed out into the street and Richard drove away. 'If he could let a little of his tension out in normal ways like slamming a door, I wouldn't be so concerned, but his control is so strong it's killing him.'

'Better him than Jackie and the kids,' Jo murmured, then, ashamed she'd even thought that way, let alone said it, she retracted it. 'No, please let's not have anyone dying.'

She looked at Cam, wondering why he was clutching beach towels against his chest.

'Did you bump into him by accident?'

'Not entirely,' Cam told her with a slow smile. 'Hence the beach towels—I wanted an excuse to come out to the van and now I'm here I'd better put them in. They won't work a second time.'

'He won't come back, surely,' Jo said, but she was still puzzled by whatever had been going on in the carport. 'Did you expect him to come?'

'I thought it was a fifty-fifty chance. Helping his wife get away was one thing, but taking his boys to the surf—that was really undermining his control of his family.'

Jo found herself sighing, something she seemed to be doing far too often these days.

'Did he mention it?'

Cam had slid open the campervan door and was putting the towels in a small cupboard under the back seat.

'Told me if they wanted to surf he'd teach them, and suggested I pass the message on to you.'

'But he was here a while, I heard the voices,' Jo said. 'Longer than delivering a message would have taken. That's why I came out. I thought it might be someone who was lost and you were having trouble with directions.'

'I tried to talk to him,' Cam admitted. 'Actually, he's got a bad shoulder and I'd just suggested he come in first thing in the morning to let me look at it.'

'And I came bumbling out and spoiled it all.'

Cam closed the door of the van and turned towards her.

'I doubt that. I don't know if I was getting through—he hadn't agreed to see me as a doctor. And for a while there, I was panicking, thinking I might have to join his cricket club and it would take up my surfing time.'

He'd have joined if he'd thought it would help Richard. The thought flashed through Jo's head and although she barely knew this man who'd come to work for her, she knew this guess had been correct. He was that kind of man.

Although…

'But would it work?' she asked. 'Even if he comes in for his shoulder, could you talk about other stuff?'

This time his smile was so warm and teasing Jo knew she should sack him right now—this very minute—and somehow muddle through the holidays on her own, or get a locum, or leave town herself. Anything rather than fall in love with Cam.

Fall in love? Where had that come from? What had happened to simple lust?

Or even complicated lust?

'What if the fact he is in pain was adding to his aggro at home?' the smiling man asked. 'And if we could do something for the pain...'

He left the sentence hanging in the air, but the way he'd said 'we' had touched off the zapping sensation along her nerves again, and she muttered a very hasty goodnight and took her bag of rubbish back into the house.

To Cam's astonishment, Richard Trent did turn up at the clinic the next morning, confirming Cam's guess that his shoulder must be extremely painful.

'Have you had ultrasound treatment before?' Cam asked him.

'A couple of years ago—maybe more. Jo's dad did it.'

The way Richard said Jo's name told Cam the man had calmed down from the anger he'd been feeling the previous evening, but Cam was also very aware he couldn't venture into any matter beyond this particular appointment.

'Then you'll probably remember that I'll put some gel on your shoulder, then rub the head of the machine across it. What it does is send sound waves into your body. They warm the area, which provides some pain relief, but more importantly they increase blood supply to the muscle or tendon to help healing and reduce swelling. Have you had an ultrasound test—same machine, different use—to pinpoint the exact problem?'

Richard was up on the treatment table by now, and Cam applied gel and moved the head of the machine over the skin of the injured shoulder.

'A while back, down in Port,' Richard admitted. 'The doctor bloke there said there was calcification in the tendons around the rotator cuff and I should have an op.'

'Maybe,' Cam told him, 'although sometimes this together with a little manipulation and massage will break the calcification down. Problem is, this treatment is best if you have it for five to ten minutes, two to three times a day. Most people can't fit three medical appointments into their day, although now you can buy small, battery-operated machines that work with the same sound waves. You could check out the local pharmacy or try the internet, maybe get one you could use at home.'

Cam finished and turned off the machine then massaged the shoulder, not talking now, knowing silence was awkward for some people and they would rush to fill it with talk.

Not Richard Trent! He remained stoically still and silent while Cam massaged his shoulder, then sat up, thanked Cam, pulled on his shirt and was preparing to depart when he hesitated.

Was Richard about to open up to him?

Remember whatever he says you have to be non-judgemental. The message rang loud and clear in Cam's head.

'I shouldn't have got upset about you taking the boys surfing—you were probably only doing what you thought was a good turn.'

Cam nodded. He wanted so desperately to help this man, and the wanting reminded him of why he'd gone further than straight medicine and studied psychology as well.

'It was nothing. I'm sorry it upset you,' he said, testing every word before he said it, afraid he could lose whatever slim connection he might have made with Richard. 'I surf every morning, and love it so much I want everyone to know the joy. I suppose it's like you with cricket. Jo was telling me you played schoolboy cricket for the state.'

'Long time ago,' Richard said. 'BM I call it.'

'BM?'

'Before marriage! Jackie was pregnant, we had

to get married, I'm not telling you anything the whole town doesn't know.'

But you're telling me you're bitter about it, very bitter, yet you've obviously been married a long time now and the abuse is only recent—what's changed? Cam's mind was racing. He knew many of the cricketers who played for their state or country were married, many with children, so why would it have stopped Richard's career?

Again speaking carefully, Cam asked, 'Would you have liked to play on? Go further?'

'Wouldn't anyone?' Richard muttered, and this time he did leave, but he left behind a man who'd received a precious gift—a reminder for Cam that this was what he enjoyed—helping people and knowing that in his own small way he *could* help people.

Not that he'd done much for Richard yet, but Cam knew he was no longer rudderless—that his career was back on track, his enthusiasm for practising medicine and psychology alive and well again.

Jo must have passed Richard in the hall, for she arrived in Cam's doorway seconds later.

'Any luck?' she asked.

Cam grinned at her.

'His shoulder *might* be less painful,' he replied, 'and I've a feeling of cautious optimism, though that could well be misplaced.'

He grinned at her, wanting to share the new optimism *he* was feeling, but she couldn't have got the vibe because she frowned, and he had a sudden urge to kiss that little frown line away.

Maybe kiss her lips as well—hold her—but not in a comforting way.

Fortunately—well, probably fortunately—she disappeared from his doorway while he was pondering kisses and hugs, leaving him staring at the space where she had been.

Puzzled and a little uneasy about this sudden urge to kiss his boss in a very inappropriate setting, he used getting a beach permit as an excuse to avoid lunch in the communal room. But was she also avoiding him that she was out at lunchtime too, and on Thursday? She actually phoned him in his consulting room on Friday to remind him of the meeting. 'I'll drive you, save taking two cars,' she suggested.

'No, I'll take the van. If we finish in time I might put my new permit to good use and go down the long beach for a surf.'

The surf had flattened out and she probably knew that, but she didn't mention it, simply reminding him the meeting was at four at the community centre.

'It's the modern-looking building behind the hospital. There's a meeting room on the left as you walk in,' she explained to him. 'See you there.'

It was fairly stupid as he couldn't avoid her for ever, and he did see her at work, passing in the hall, meeting to discuss a patient at the front desk, but in work mode he could forget how she'd looked on a surfboard, body curved, head held high, eyes aglow, at one with the elemental force of the ocean—in control of the curling green wave.

Almost forget.

He was early for the meeting—army training too strong for him to ever arrive anywhere late. But arriving early had its own reward, for he could see these virtual strangers enter the room, and watch the interaction between them.

Mike was an organiser, arriving with a small briefcase that he opened to reveal a laptop and a sheaf of papers, copies of an agenda, Cam discovered when Mike handed him one.

Lauren, now, was different. One look at her face when Tom walked in was enough to tell Cam she was attracted to his old acquaintance, which made the fact that Tom studiously avoided looking at Lauren even more interesting. Lauren was a beautiful woman, and Tom was a man who collected beautiful women. Had he tried and been rebuffed?

The attraction between them seemed apparent to Cam, a newcomer, looking in from the outside, but one was resisting and one was ignoring—interesting!

'Did you come to try the chairs or are you going to get involved?'

Jo's teasing remark brought him out of his analysis of the vibes in the room and he smiled at the people he was finding so intriguing.

'Thinking of something,' he said, then knew he'd made a mistake. Jo wasn't one to let an opening like that slip away.

'So tell,' she demanded, and Cam had to sort some vague thoughts he'd had while out on his board this morning into sensible order. But not before he'd snapped a 'Yes, boss' and a crisp salute at her, and watched the delicious colour rise in her cheeks.

Business! his head reminded him.

'I think long term we—or you lot—need to get the men's programme up and running, and we can start planning it and working on how best to get men to attend. As far as attendance goes, we can contact people who already run these programmes to see if they've any ideas. But...'

He paused, aware he had their attention.

'While outlining what we're doing to get that up and running *might* impress the people who hold the purse-strings, maybe another project, one we could begin right now, would show we're serious about running an integrated programme against domestic violence in the Cove. For a start, get the local council involved. I've noticed as I've travelled north that many towns have big signs on the highway where the town begins, saying domestic violence isn't tolerated in this town, and a toll-free number to call for help.'

'That's a great idea,' Lauren told him. 'I'll get on to the council.'

'Actually, I can do that. I'll talk to the mayor about it,' Cam offered.

Jo was smiling at him—like a teacher pleased with her pupil?—but she wasn't letting him stop there.

'And?' she prompted.

'We should begin awareness programmes in the high schools—right now. This time of year, the final-year students have gone, but the lower years are still there and teachers are at their wits' end, trying to keep their pupils occupied. I know this because army recruitment officers were always welcomed at the end of term time. We could offer to do a school programme focussing on violence.'

Jo caught on first.

'You're right. We need to get kids, especially adolescents, not only aware of DV but thinking seriously about how they handle anger. What do they see of violence? How do they think about it? How does it make them feel? We could do some role playing of appropriate and inappropriate be-haviour, get the kids involved, the older ones in doing role plays and the younger ones making posters.'

'We started working on something like that last year,' Lauren said, looking directly at Tom for the first time, and colouring slightly.

Definitely something there, Cam confirmed to himself.

'Just before schoolies,' Tom offered. 'Then all hell broke loose. We had that low off the coast, gale-force winds and rain, and some of the kids' tents were blown away and both the hospital and the refuge became hostels for wet, stranded teen-agers.'

'Better weather forecast for this year,' Mike said, but in such gloomy tones Cam *had* to ask.

'Are they so bad, the schoolies? After all, they're legally adults, most of them. They're over eigh-teen when they leave school. Surely they don't all run wild?'

'Wait and see,' Jo warned him, green eyes pin-ning him in place—distracting him. 'Explain-ing schoolies is impossible, although, as an army man, maybe you can imagine it. Picture a couple of hundred new recruits turned loose for a week, alcohol flowing freely—binge drinking is appar-ently what you do to prove you're an adult—some drugs, although Mike and his crew are very vigi-lant and we have a great sniffer dog wandering through the gatherings, and then there are hor-monal girls and testosterone-laden youths and all the problems of love and lust.'

Cam rather wished she hadn't mentioned tes-tosterone and lust, but he set that distraction aside to concentrate on what he was learning.

'We have a chill-out zone staffed with volunteers where kids feeling sick or lost or just in need of a hug can go. We have bottled water available all over the place, the council provides entertainment on the esplanade, local and imported bands, most nights, and generally speaking we're really well prepared and organised,' Lauren said, and Cam heard the but hanging at the end of the sentence.

'Anyway, let's tackle schoolies when we have to. For now, can we discuss Cam's idea?' Jo said. 'He's right in thinking we'd be welcomed at the high school. Lauren, have you got time to work with him on a rough outline for a programme? And maybe the two of you could do the first run, then whoever is available could do the other classes. I think having a man and a woman running each session makes it easier to do some simulated violence scenes and maybe if there's time, we could talk about control issues as well—equate it to bullying, which is a big issue in schools these days.'

So, Jo's palming me off onto Lauren, and from the look on Tom's face he's no happier about it than I am, Cam realised.

Than I am?

For crying out loud, what was happening to him?

I'm going soft on my boss, that's what, he admitted to himself, and for some bizarre reason the admission sent a rush of heat through his body.

Jo was watching Cam's face and, no, she wasn't going to think about why her gaze had drifted that way, so she saw his reaction to her suggestion about him working with Lauren.

Puzzled? Yes, puzzlement was there, but also present was something that looked like suspicion. She hadn't deliberately suggested they work together, had she?

Of course not, she'd suggested it because they both had psychology training so were the best suited for the job. Of course, Lauren *was* beautiful, and Jo had felt for a long time that Lauren needed a man in her life. No harm in bumping them together.

No harm at all and the squelchy feeling inside her at that thought actually confirmed it was a good idea. She'd had enough internal disturbances over Fraser Cameron.

'We need get the programme organised first,' Lauren suggested, then she smiled at Cam. 'Your boss ever give you time off? If we're going to put our heads together, it would suit me better during the day. With the cutbacks in funding I'm doing the night shift at the refuge. It's not a late night for me, but after it I'm too drained to do any logical thinking.'

Cam turned to Jo and raised his eyebrows.

'Tell me what time suits you, Lauren, and Cam can fit in,' Jo said. 'I didn't know I'd have help this week so I'm palming patients off to him as they come in. We haven't written any appointments up for him so far, so he wouldn't be breaking any.'

Lauren mentioned a time, and Jo ran very efficiently through all the decisions they'd made and the jobs people had to do, listing Cam as the person to get in touch with people running existing men's programmes and telling Lauren that as the chairman of the co-ordinating domestic violence scheme in the Cove she, Jo, would handle the applications for funding.

'I think,' she added, the little frown that creased her brow—one line only—attracting Cam's attention, 'that we have to rename ourselves. Being just a co-ordinating committee for the refuge has been fine up to now, but I think we need to show the funding bodies that we're serious. We need to show we're being proactive in dealing with domestic violence throughout the community, which is what we'll be doing.'

'How about the Domestic Violence Integrated Response Team?' Mike suggested, showing Cam by his use of key words that he was an old hand at filling out forms for government agencies.

'Not sure about the "Response",' Tom said. 'Jo's right, we've got to go beyond responding to situations if we want to prove our worth.'

'Response and Prevention?' Lauren offered. 'After all, we do a lot of work with women to show them how to stay safe in their relationships.'

'Let's think about it,' Jo said. 'We're on the right track and we've enough to go on with for now. But while we're here, can we get back to schoolies? Mike, have you got enough volunteers for the chill-out zone?'

'We've got the usual lot but can always use more.'

He turned to Cam.

'You going to volunteer, mate?' he asked. 'Up to now, Tom and Jo have shared the call-out duties.'

'Happy to do it,' Cam said. 'I imagine Jo can tell me where to be and when. She's good that way, my boss.'

Jo decided to ignore him, although she'd heard

the tease behind the words. Had anyone else heard it? Would it start speculation?

Not that there was anything to speculate on.

And why would that depress her?

'Let's all go to the pub for a bite to eat,' she suggested, thinking a relaxing beer and a little light conversation with her friends might restore her equilibrium.

'You'll have to count me out,' Tom said. 'I've a patient coming in from a farm up in the hills, suspected broken collarbone. He'll be arriving any minute.'

'And I'm on duty at the refuge,' Lauren said, 'much as I'd have loved a relaxing evening with friends.'

Whether Mike was going to join them became a moot point when he answered his mobile.

'Road accident,' he said briefly. 'No injuries but both drivers over the limit.'

He left the room as Tom also stood up and closed the file he'd had in front of him. He was watching Lauren as she, too, stood and Jo could see the concern on Tom's face. He was as worried as she, Jo, was, about Lauren's health. Her friend was driving herself to exhaustion.

'I can do some evenings at the refuge,' Jo offered. 'Now I've got another doctor in the practice, I'm not nearly as busy, and Cam could take any late calls that come in if I'm not available.'

'I can manage,' Lauren said.

'Not for much longer,' Jo told her. 'And I'm telling you that as your doctor as well as your friend.'

Lauren sighed. She waited until Tom had followed Mike out of the room, then said quietly, 'You haven't heard, have you?'

'Heard what?' Jo asked.

'Nat Williams is coming home for Christmas. Bringing his American wife and their two kids—they'll be here for a month.'

Jo was so shocked by Lauren's attitude she forgot a stranger—well, almost stranger—was in the room with them.

'You can't possibly still be carrying a torch for that man,' she fumed. 'Lauren, get over it—it was, what, nearly fifteen years ago?'

'I am *not* carrying a torch for him,' Lauren said. 'His dumping me was the best thing he ever did for me. It's not that, it's the family thing, coming here with his wife...'

She shrugged her too-thin shoulders.

'I can't explain it. You know me—practical

Lauren—never one to go for vague feelings but the feeling I have isn't vague and I don't even know if it's to do with Nat. Maybe it's the refuge and the trouble we're in there, or—oh, I don't know, Jo, I hate sounding melodramatic and you know that isn't like me, but I have this terrible sense of impending doom.'

CHAPTER EIGHT

'WELL, on that cheerful note,' Cam said brightly, shattering the tension that had wound around them in the room, 'perhaps you and I, Jo, can adjourn to the pub. Best place to prepare for doom, surely. I'll drink squash and do any night calls. Sure you can't join us, just for a meal?'

He was asking Lauren, who'd regained a little of the colour she'd lost as she'd made her strange confession.

She smiled at him—he was a man who could make women smile, Jo realised—and shook her head.

'Not tonight but I'll take a rain-check,' she told him, then she smiled again and in a softer voice said, 'Thanks, Cam.'

Maybe if she pushed a little, the two of them could get together, Jo decided, ignoring the squelchy feeling, smothering it under an unspoken assertion that this was a noble thing she was doing, finding Lauren such a nice man.

'Impending doom?' Cam queried as Jo packed up her bits of paper, shoving them willy-nilly into a file. Considering her house and what he'd seen of her office, he didn't think she was the willy-nilly type, so...

'Don't tell me *you're* picking up on Lauren's foreboding?' he asked her.

Her head snapped up and she frowned at him.

'Why on earth would you think that?'

He grinned at her.

'The way you're shovelling papers into your file. Everything I've seen of you suggests a person who likes things tidy—meticulous—and that's not meticulous behaviour.'

'Well, thanks!' she snapped, then she muttered, 'Meticulous behaviour indeed,' under her breath.

'Well?' he demanded, when they reached the car park where their vehicles stood side by side.

'Well what?' she was frowning again but this time she seemed genuinely puzzled.

'Are you concerned about impending doom?'

She shook her head, then sighed again.

'I *am* concerned about Lauren,' she admitted. 'I have been for some time. She works too hard and she worries too much. We all feel inadequate from time to time, especially when it comes to the women we help, but Lauren takes it more to heart, somehow.'

'As if it's personal? Did she grow up in an abusive home?'

Jo looked up at him, her eyes, silvery-green tonight, widening in surprise.

'Lauren? No way. Her parents were lovely—still are. They run cattle on a property up in the hills behind the town, a farm that's been in the family for generations.'

She paused, then added, 'And I know that a lot of abuse does go on in rural areas and that most of it goes unnoticed so it's unreported, but I stayed with Lauren often enough when I was a kid to know that her father was the gentlest of men. No, there's no hidden violence in her background.'

Jo was very convinced, and reasonably convincing, but Cam had recognised the signs of extreme tension in Lauren and if her experience of abuse hadn't come from her family, that left…

Some boyfriend in her past?

Not Nat Williams, surely!

Not the golden boy of Australian surfing?

Lauren would have been away from the Cove while she was studying—down in Sydney, he guessed. Maybe something had happened there.

But she'd mentioned Nat Williams's return…

'Are you waiting for some sign that you should open your car door? A green flash in the sky? Three crows on a wire? A pelican flying backwards?'

Jo's gentle tease made him realise he was standing by his van, key in the driver's door, fingers on the key, completely lost in contemplation.

'Would Nat Williams have hit her?'

He hadn't meant to ask. It had been nothing more than a continuation of his thoughts, but he'd spoken it aloud.

Jo's 'Nat?' was so disbelieving he knew he'd guessed wrong, until she followed it with a soft 'Oh!' She shook her head and her eyes looked into his with bewilderment and maybe just a little fear.

'Surely not,' Jo added, horrified, pushing away the possibility, but not far enough.

'Surely I'd have known,' she said, watching Cam's face, desperately seeking some kind of answer there. 'Or Lauren would have told me?'

'Would she?' Cam asked gently.

Jo took a deep, steadying breath.

'Given what I now know about domestic violence, probably not,' she admitted. 'When I first got involved with the refuge, I was astounded at how quiet the women kept it, as if they were to blame for it and so were too ashamed to talk about it.'

'Usually the abuser has convinced them they *are* to blame,' Cam reminded her.

'You're right,' Jo told him, despair killing off any last remnants of the upbeat feeling the positive meeting had produced. 'There's also the issue that if they do tell someone close to them, more often than not the person they tell doesn't believe them. Look at Jackie. I know for a fact that her parents think Richard's a fantastic guy. He played schoolboy cricket for the state and Jackie's father is a cricket fanatic so he loves Richard like a son. If she mentioned to them that he hit her, her parents would immediately wonder what she'd done to deserve it.'

She slumped against her car, and bent her head, drawing circles in the sandy car park with the toe of her sandals.

'Sometimes it seems so hopeless,' she said.

'Never!' Cam said firmly. 'All you need is a hug, then you'll pick yourself up and soldier on. I know enough of you by now to understand you're not a quitter. You're just letting Lauren's sense of doom cloud you at the moment.'

And on that note he proceeded to prise her off the car and enfold her in a warm, hard hug. A super-hug if hugs could have ratings, because his body was so firm and well muscled, so warm, his arms so all-enveloping, and she could rest her cheek against his heart and let all the tension of the day flow out of her.

She could also feel his heartbeat, strong, and regular, as vital as the man himself, and given that it was a very comfortable position she indulged herself and stayed a little longer than she probably should have. After all, she was giving him to Lauren and this might be her last opportunity to enjoy a super-hug.

He shouldn't have done it. Cam knew that immediately. He shouldn't have touched her. He should never touch her because it started his libido shouting about the other things he wanted to do to her, like press his lips against that blue vein at her temple, and kiss her just there at the nape of her neck on the bit of pale skin he saw when her hair was up, and eventually he would slide his lips around her neck, and finish on her tempting pink mouth.

And he'd like to run his hands across her back, feeling the bones beneath the skin of this woman who was getting beneath his own skin. There were other bits of her he'd like to touch and kiss as well, but he definitely wasn't going to think of those now, just give her the comforting friend-and-colleague hug he knew she needed and leave it at that.

But she seemed happy in the hug so he held on, pressing her body against his, feeling her warmth, wondering if it was because she'd had so much anguish in her life with her sister's accident that she was attuned to unhappiness in others. If so, it would make her doubly anxious about Lauren.

He tightened his hold on her but only out of sympathy…

'I think perhaps hugging in the community centre car park isn't the best thing to be doing late on a Friday afternoon, seeing that hospital visitors use it and visiting hours are just finishing.'

She eased out of his arms as she spoke, and looked up at him, her face so delicately flushed, her eyes so intriguingly puzzled—what had just happened? they seemed to ask—he wanted to hug her again.

To be perfectly honest, he wanted to hug her again for other reasons, but best he didn't consider them right now.

'Pub?' he asked.

She nodded, then said, 'Come in my car, I can drop you back at the van later.'

Strewth, but she was a bossy woman!

'Not tonight,' he told her. 'I'm the one drinking squash. The van might rattle a bit but it's very comfortable. Before I bought it, the whole thing had been restored by this chap who had a passion for the old original campervans. He'd even re-upholstered the seats.'

Jo didn't seem convinced, climbing into the van and looking dubiously around her.

'A bench seat?' she queried, when Cam got in beside her.

'That's what all the original vans had,' he assured her, not adding that he'd always thought bench seats far better than single seats in vehicles. He wanted to point out that it had a seat belt for a person to sit in the middle, thinking how nice it would be to drive with Jo pressed up against him, but she'd already buckled herself into place beside the door—a million miles away, or so it seemed.

Not that there was any reason for her to be closer. Intellectually he knew that. Physically—well, as far as he was concerned, she could never sit *too* close.

Never?

Was he thinking—?

'If you turn left as you come out of the gates,' the person he wanted sitting closer to him said, her voice so matter-of-fact he knew she wasn't thinking about closeness, 'we'll go to the middle pub. You've probably noticed it, the two-storey one with the iron lace around the top balcony.'

'And the old swing doors downstairs? I've walked past it and wondered that they'd kept them. Most pubs took them out before I was born, I imagine for security reasons as much as for updating their look.'

He glanced towards her and saw a little smile quirking the corners of her mouth.

'I suspect they weren't original to this particular place, but were brought in at some time when the place was undergoing renovation to give it the old-time look it has. There are steel grilles that are lowered to secure the doorways after hours—spoils the look altogether—but for all that, it does the best meals of the three pubs.'

He drove down to the esplanade and found a parking spot almost opposite the pub, but when he pulled into it, neither of them moved. *He* was watching the way the waves rolled up the beach, seeking out the surfers on the point break closer to the headland, checking out the waves.

Was Jo also watching them? Thinking of the thrill getting back on a board had given her? Would she—?

'The forecast is good for the morning, tide coming in and a good swell, offshore winds later. I usually go out at about five-thirty, just as dawn is breaking. Want to come?'

She turned towards him but the shadows in the van made it impossible to read her face, and he couldn't guess what he was thinking.

'Stupid, isn't it?' she finally declared. 'I'm sure a psychiatrist would say I'm denying myself the joy of surfing as some kind of punishment for Jill's accident, but at the time, well, all I wanted was to be with her whenever I could, and I got out of the habit of surfing every day.'

'I doubt a *good* psychiatrist would tell you that,' he said carefully. 'Sometimes we humans over-analyse things that happen. We look back and try to find meanings in them because we can't accept that often things just happen—there *is* no meaning. But since you've been back living at the Cove, you've not wanted to surf?'

Cam held his breath as he watched her considering the situation.

If she gave in and started surfing again, would she also give in on relationships, something else he was reasonably sure she'd been denying herself?

Then, with a little shake of her head, she said, 'Actually, I run in the mornings these days. It not only keeps me fit but it gives me time to think about the day ahead and plan what needs to be done.'

She slid out of the van, shut the door with care, and walked around to the rear where she waited until he'd locked the doors and joined her. He took her elbow to walk across the street—surely that level of polite touching was permissible in a boss-employee relationship even if his motivations weren't quite as gentlemanly as the act itself.

Damn it all! What was he thinking? He had to get thoughts of Jo as anything *but* his boss right out of his head. As she never tired of reminding him, he wasn't staying, and even on such short acquaintance he was certain she wasn't a woman who would enjoy a brief, no-strings affair. On top of which, he knew he wasn't ready for a relationship himself, although—

The 'although' brought him up short. It had certainly been hours, perhaps even a full day, since he'd had memory flashes of the carnage in the building where the young soldiers had been, certainly days since he'd replayed in his head some of the conversations he'd had with those who'd survived.

And then there was the satisfaction he'd felt this morning, treating Richard—the return of his confidence in himself as a doctor, as someone who could help another human being through tough times.

Maybe...

They entered through the swing doors and Jo led him through another door into a wood-panelled dining room, complete with crisp white linen tablecloths, small silver vases, each holding a single rose, and old-fashioned glass and silver salt and pepper shakers in a silver cruet.

'They certainly carried through with the olden-days feel for the place,' he said, as they slid into chairs at a table for two in the far corner of the room. It was a quiet corner, away from a family group at a larger table and another table where two couples were laughing as they discussed some mishap that had befallen one of their party.

The menus were in a rack and Jo picked one up but didn't open it, looking at him instead, a serious expression on her face.

'What form does your baggage take?' She frowned and shook her head. 'That sounded wrong, but I know about baggage and how we shut it away in dark corners of our minds, but does yours recur in some way so you realise it isn't really shut away at all?'

He found it hard to believe she could ask the question out of the blue when he'd been thinking about it as they'd crossed the road, but he didn't believe people could read each other's minds, so it had to be coincidence.

You don't have to answer her, his head told him, but the anxiety he could read in her face contradicted that.

'I get flashes of images in my head and hear scraps of conversation,' he admitted. 'I hear young soldiers telling me they can't take any more, or crying as they admit to being scared. The voices are worse than the images, although the images are of brutally injured bodies. They bring out all the usual symptoms—cold sweats, racing heart, minor panic attacks—great stuff for a doctor to be experiencing, although I *can* assure you it never happens when I'm with a patient.'

She reached out and touched his hand where it lay on the open menu.

'I wondered because I had images as well, usually at the most—not exactly inappropriate time but at weird times. I'd be really involved in something that bore no relation to the accident, and suddenly I'd see Jill's body picked up by the wave and flung towards the cliff. And although with the crashing of the waves I'm quite sure I didn't hear her cry out, I used to hear this desperate yell...'

Cam watched her chest rise and he knew she was taking a deep breath.

'You must think I'm crazy, coming out with the question—telling you this stuff—but I wanted to say that although you never forget—it's always with you—in time the images fade and the cries become fainter.' She shrugged her shoulders and he saw that delicate flush that fascinated him rise again in her cheeks. 'It probably won't help you, your own experiences must have been so cataclysmic compared to an injured sister, but I thought I'd say it anyway.'

She moved her hand, but he caught it, and squeezed her fingers, feeling his chest grow tight at the same time.

'I'm glad you said it. Thank you, Jo.'

Her fingers moved in his, returning his clasp, and Cam felt he'd like the moment to last for ever—to just sit and hold Jo's hand in his.

For ever…

CHAPTER NINE

ON SATURDAY the schoolies arrived and Cam, wandering down town after the medical centre had closed at midday, was astounded to see the action. Large cars pulling up to disgorge teenagers, luggage and cartons of beer and spirit mixes. Teenagers everywhere, mostly roving in packs, tents springing up like colourful, exotic fungi in the caravan park, high fences up along the esplanade and a stage erected where the bands would perform.

He found the chill-out zone, already staffed by a young policeman who was handing out wristbands to anyone who wanted them.

'Wristbands?' Cam queried after he'd introduced himself.

'All schoolies must be wearing one to gain entry into the fenced areas. We personalise them, using indelible markers that won't wash off in water. We print their best friend's mobile number in blue and a phone number for their family in red. The red is for emergencies should one of them be hurt, but if the person is just lost or a bit under the weather, we call the friend.'

'Great idea,' Cam said, looking around the fenced area with its chairs and rugs and cushions, the stacked boxes of bottle water, a stack of buckets—for people who were sick?—wet paper towels, dry towels and a locked medicine chest.

'Do the kids use this place?' he asked.

The young policeman nodded.

'Just you wait and see. It's not so busy during the day, usually just kids wanting directions or programmes, but at night the volunteers are flat out. Right now the volunteers are out there, giving out pamphlets that explain what's available at the chill-out zone and a list of phone numbers for emergencies.'

'Very organised,' Cam said, but as the mass of young people continued to expand he began to wonder just what lay ahead of him in the week to come.

He didn't have to wonder long. On duty in the zone that evening, the sun had barely set and the bands were thumping out their beats when two young women came in, their friend, agitated and babbling excitedly but not making any sense, held between them.

'She just got all twitchy and hyper,' one of them explained, while Cam helped the woman onto one of the couches in the zone and bent to examine her.

He couldn't smell alcohol on her breath, but she felt hot to the touch and her pulse was erratic. He loosened her clothing, asking at the same time, 'Has she taken anything?'

One of the girls immediately said no, but the other one looked uncomfortable.

'Here,' he said, handing the uncomfortable one a bottle of water. 'I'll sit her up and you give her sips of water.'

He turned to the second friend.

'You can wet one of those small towels and wipe it over her skin to cool her down, *and*—' he looked directly at her as he emphasised the word '—you can tell me what she took.'

'It was only an E,' the friend replied, hurrying to obey Cam, adding, when she returned, 'She's had them before. She *brought* them for us so they were hers, not bought here off some stranger.'

As if that made it all right, Cam thought wryly.

'Been dancing a lot?' he asked, and the two girls

nodded, while their sick friend began to moan and shake. Cam grabbed a bucket, held it while she was sick, then shoved it under a table, thinking he'd have to find out about disposal later. There were three chemical toilet stalls at the back of the zone but he wasn't sure if they were suitable for handling the bucket's contents.

The patient was obviously feeling better, although still pale and shaky.

'Keep drinking water. You're dehydrated and you're very silly to be taking any kind of drug. You've, all three of you, got such a wonderful life in front of you, you don't want to be risking it with something that could kill you and, believe me, badly cut drugs *can* kill people and you've obviously got hold of some Ecstasy that's been badly cut.'

He left them sitting on the couch, looking more scared than penitent, but scared was good. He delved amongst the well-labelled plastic boxes of supplies. Found what he was looking for, some rehydrating salts in tablet form that dissolved to make a palatable drink.

'You drink this,' he told his patient. 'Then rest here for a while. Your friends might like to go back to the concert and come by later to take you back to where you're staying.'

The young woman looked at her friends, who both leant down to give her a hug.

'We'll stick with you,' they said in unison, one adding, 'It's what we promised each other. Anyway, we can hear the bands okay from here— down there on the beach they're far too loud.'

'That's a job well done,' Cam heard a voice say as he left the girls together on the couch. 'And I've emptied and cleaned out the bucket for you,' Jo added, smiling at him and pointing to where she'd stacked the disinfected bucket. 'In case you were wondering, you *can* empty them into the toilets. Apparently the chemicals they use can cope with anything.'

She moved into the light and he noticed she was wearing a dress for the first time since they'd met. Well, almost wearing a dress for it was a very skimpy mini, all frills and tiny flowers and so unlike Jo's usual uniform of khaki shorts and tank tops Cam was aware he did a classic double-take.

'You look fantastic!'

The words were out before he'd had time to

consider them but she didn't seem to mind, giving him a half-wry smile.

'Not my usual style at all, is it?' she said, but she gave a twirl that suggested she was enjoying the difference. 'Actually, it's my schoolies' gear. Look around at what the young women are wearing. In this dress I fit in, and I can wander through the crowds without attracting too much attention.'

'Yes?' Cam said, his eyebrows rising. 'I would think in that gear you'd get all the attention you can handle and probably more. Why the need to wander? Are you the second sniffer dog?'

Jo grinned at him and he felt a spurt of heat in his veins.

'More or less,' she answered. 'I just mooch around and listen so if anything's going on—like a whisper that you can get dope behind the clubhouse kind of thing—we're prepared. A number of the younger lifesavers do it as well, two young couples and another teenager, mingling with the crowds. The problem isn't the schoolies but the lot they call toolies—men usually, a couple of years out of school—who come back each year, some just to hang around but others who could be predators, on the lookout for girls who've had too much to drink and have lost their caution.'

Revulsion now coiled where heat had been.

'Rape?' Cam asked.

'We had one report last year but the young woman couldn't remember what the man looked like, except that he looked older. She left the enclosed area in front of the stage to walk along the beach with him. It was low tide and he took her in behind rocks near the headland. It was two days before her friends persuaded her to tell someone in the chill-out zone and by then it was too late to do anything apart from helping her over the experience. This year we're being more proactive, being more insistent that the young people look out for their buddy or buddies.'

'And you're walking around as shark bait?' Cam suggested, distinctly uneasy at the thought of Jo out there asking for trouble.

Jo shook her head.

'It's fairly obvious to anyone on the lookout for an easy mark that I'm not eighteen, but it doesn't hurt to have people wandering through the crowd.'

She waltzed away, leaving Cam feeling very disturbed, especially as she'd no sooner left the zone than a couple of young men hit on her. He watched as she laughed and joked with them, then moved on, apparently convincing them she wasn't interested in their company.

Was he concerned about her?

The thought brought a tingling sensation crawling up Jo's spine and she probably smiled too warmly at the two young men who approached her as she left the zone. They didn't seem too unhappy when she refused their invitation to the pub, probably realising she was older than she'd looked as they'd approached her.

But if Cam was concerned about her…

Of course, it was probably just in a boss-employee way, so she should forget the tingles, although…

She mooched through the crowd of teenagers, feeling very old among them, aware it was okay to look the part, but she no longer knew the passwords of acceptance—the speech patterns and 'in' words, even what band was hot and what was not.

Two hours later, feeling fairly confident that all was well this first night of the five the schoolies would be in residence, she returned to the zone to find Cam still there, not tending a patient but sitting chatting to a couple of young men. The words *barrelling* and *shore breaks* told her the conversation was about surfing so she didn't intrude, although when the visitors left he waved her over.

'Have a seat,' he suggested. 'You look as if you've been dancing the night away.'

He passed her a bottle of water, their fingers touching, almost lingering together, as he passed it.

It's not happening, she told herself, denying the signals from her body, sending the moon a dirty look—moon-madness.

'How did you go?' Cam asked as she finished a long draught of water and set the bottle down on the grass.

'I'm far too old to do the mingling thing any more,' she told him. 'For a start, it's as if they speak a foreign language and this habit young people have developed of throwing the word *like* into every sentence makes me want to bang my head against a wall.'

She leant down to pick up the water bottle and had another drink while she settled not her thoughts but her feelings. Surely if she could sit here and carry on a sensible conversation with Cam, her skin would stop sending messages about how close he was.

'It's not that I'm not used to it but on the whole teenagers who come as patients are on their best behaviour, speaking the language their parents speak, not teenage-speak, while as for noise levels—I mean we're, what, five hundred metres away from the stage and even here the ground seems to shake with the thrum of the deep bass notes. Closer to it, inside the fenced area, I needed ear plugs.'

She was giving herself a metaphorical pat on the back for the sensible conversation when Cam moved, just slightly, but enough for his thigh to rest against hers as they sat together on the couch. Just the touch of a thigh, and sensible was destroyed, her mind considering the ridiculous suggestions her body was making.

A brief affair—surely that would be okay? A fling—that's all it would be. He was moving on, so nothing serious, and wasn't it okay to enjoy physical pleasure just for its own sake?

The worst of it was that, as her thigh positively revelled in the closeness of his, her mind didn't seem to be coming up with any answers. It certainly wasn't pouring cold water on the ideas her body was suggesting.

Or even lukewarm water.

Not a murmur from the common sense on which she prided herself.

She moved her thigh—that was commonsense, wasn't it?

Unfortunately, Cam turned at the same time, and his hand fell onto her knee, a casual gesture, no pressure, but she felt the imprint of his fingers searing like a brand into her skin. A momentary regret that she wasn't in her usual cargo shorts was swamped when his fingers *did* exert pressure, and he nodded towards the gate of the chill-out zone where three young men were trying to control their obviously drunk and loudly obnoxious friend.

'Do we take drunks?' Cam asked, standing up and moving in front of Jo in case the young man lurched towards her.

'Mildly drunk, yes,' Jo told him, moving out of his protective shadow, 'but guys like that we give to Mike and his boys. They let them dry out in one of their cells where they can't do any harm to themselves or others.'

She nodded towards the young policeman, in

casual dress but still on duty in the zone. He was on his mobile, obviously calling for a car. Once the call was finished, the policeman herded the young men out of the zone to wait by the road, his grip on the drunk man not particularly gentle but definitely effective.

Cam was about to ask if someone kept an eye on the drunks in the cells when a cry from the beach told him there was more trouble.

'Help, please help!'

A woman's voice, high, hysterical.

Jo moved with him but his longer strides ate up the distance across the sand to where a group of young people huddled around a supine form. One of the young men was on his knees, pressing at the unconscious woman's chest, and although his compressions might not have been copybook, Cam congratulated the boy on his fast action as he explained who he was and knelt to take over.

Within seconds Jo was there as well.

'No pulse yet,' she said, her fingers beneath the young woman's chin. 'I'll count and do the breaths,' she told him, and so they worked together. In between breaths, Jo pressed a button on her mobile then handed it to one of the onlookers.

'That will ring through to the ambulance station. Please tell them we need them on the beach just north of the band area.'

And with that taken care of with her usual efficiency, she told the youth beside her to take over the counting, breathed three times into their patient's mouth, and this time as she looked up she began to ask questions.

'What happened?'

There was a group shuffle in reply, then one of the young women spoke up.

'We were only paddling on the edge, going in up to our knees.'

'Great timing—dusk and dawn are the very best times to get taken by a shark, but as she's still here, that couldn't have happened, so what did?'

'She just dived under a wave and didn't come up.'

The voice was familiar and now Cam looked up, then back down at their patient.

'You're the girl who was at the zone earlier,' he said to the explainer. 'And this is your friend—the one you were supposed to take back to wherever you're staying.'

The young woman hung her head, but the second friend now stepped forward.

'We *did* go back to our motel,' she protested. 'We even got ready for bed, that's why we're in different clothes, then Jodie…' she indicated her friend on the sand '…said she felt better and what she really wanted was a walk on the beach in the moonlight and we didn't know she'd go diving in like that.'

'Pulse,' Jo said, just as two ambos arrived, a folded stretcher held under the arm of the leader.

The paramedics took over, while Jo put her arms around the two friends, asking them to come back to the zone, telling them they needed a hot drink, but probably, Cam guessed, so they could get details about the patient.

'Is it like this every night?' he asked Jo, when a second wave of volunteers arrived at one in the morning to take over from the early shift.

'Most nights,' Jo told him. 'Although by the end of the five days they're here they're getting pretty tired and not as many go raging on the beach.'

She was outside the zone, leaning against the fence, looking as if she was too tired to even make it to her car. The frilly dress was still wet from where she'd held and comforted the young woman who'd pulled her friend from the water, and it clung to her body, provoking thoughts Cam was far too tired to do anything about.

'Come on, I'll drive you home,' he suggested. He put his arm around her shoulders and tucked her close. 'I was here quite early so I found a parking spot right behind the zone. Don't argue. I can run you back down in the morning to get your car, or in the afternoon, or whenever you like.'

Jo melted against him.

He was so solid, so comforting that for a fleeting moment she wondered how it would feel to let go of all the burdens she carried—let Cam carry them. No, that wouldn't be fair as he had burdens of his own—but maybe let him share them.

As if he'd want them.

Want her.

He walked her to the van, unlocked the passenger door, opened it for her then, to her surprise, lifted her as easily as she could lift a child, and deposited her on the seat. She was still getting over her sheer astonishment at this behaviour when he leaned in to do up her seat belt—somehow she was sitting in the middle of the bench— and with that task completed, he dropped a quick kiss on her lips.

Aren't we even going to talk about this? she wondered. He's just going to put me where he wants me, kiss me on the lips and…

And what?

What did it mean?

It wasn't as if it had been a passionate kiss. In fact, if anything, it had been a casual peck, nothing more, which still didn't explain his easing her into the middle seat.

Where her thigh was again, now he was behind the wheel, pressed to his.

It took the drive home—not a long drive but long enough—for her to get this far in her thought processes, but when he stopped, not in the carport but just off the road above the drive where they could look out over the town and the moonstruck ocean, she finally regained enough equilibrium to speak.

'And what was that about?' she asked. Unfortunately, by now he'd looped his arm around her shoulder and drawn her right up against her body.

'What was what about?'

Oh, he was smooth, this man—rich, dark-chocolate images tumbled through her head.

'That kiss!' she muttered crossly, furious with herself for letting him…not exactly manipulate her but make her think things she hadn't ever thought before.

He turned her towards him.

'*That* wasn't a kiss,' he said, and she could hear the smile in his voice, although she was desperately trying to look out to sea—to look anywhere rather than at his face—

'*This* is a kiss.'

His mouth closed on hers, his lips moulding themselves to hers. There was strength in his lips, or maybe not strength but sureness, as if they knew exactly how to kiss her to draw out the response they wanted.

Not that lips could make decisions. This fuzzy thought flitted by as Jo found herself losing any vestige of control she might have had over the kissing situation. Her lips were kissing him back. They were pressing so hard against his she could feel his teeth, and now his tongue traced the outline of her mouth, a subtle manoeuvre that she soon realised was a prelude to invasion.

Warm and sweet! Cam knew she'd taste like this and he revelled in it, thinking nectar, bees—no bees were wrong. The buzzing was in his head—maybe in his body—definitely in his blood…

He deepened the kiss, letting his lips speak

without words, drawing a response that added to his excitement because it told him she wanted this as much as he did.

Inexplicable attraction but lack of explanation made it no less real.

Thrumming now, his blood, taking up the beat of the music they'd heard earlier, slow and heavy, his body all but erupting into flames with his need for her.

'We can't do this.'

The whispered words lacked so much conviction he had to laugh.

'No?' he whispered back, his hand finding her breast beneath the frilly dress, cupping it, thumb and forefinger teasing at her nipple.

'No,' she answered, and gave lie to the answer by pressing closer to him, so he could feel the reverberations from the kiss quivering in her body, her nipples pebbling beneath his questing fingers.

Her reactions heightened his need and he shifted in his seat, common sense dictating they go inside to finish off what they—or he—had started, but in moving he might lose her. Besides, he wasn't done with kissing yet, particularly as he'd discovered that kissing Jo banished all the darkness from inside his head, leaving it clear and light and filled with...

Joy?

He didn't know that he'd ever been exactly filled with joy, so perhaps it *was* joy, he just didn't recognise it.

His roaming hand dropped to her waist, feeling the indentation of it, firm muscle beneath the skin on her belly—she was fit, this pint-sized boss of his, but now he wanted to see her naked. Pictured her, firm, and pale, and beautiful.

Her hands were on his face, cupping it, easing it away—easing their lips apart.

'It's not that I'm against kissing in the front seat of a campervan,' she murmured, her voice just breathless enough to tweak Cam's excitement higher, 'but we're out in public—almost—and doctors are supposed to be held in some esteem, particularly in small towns.'

He could see her face in the moonlight, see the scattering of freckles across her nose and cheeks, see lips puffy with his kisses and in her cheeks the rosiness of—what?

Embarrassment?

Desire?

He had no idea, and the realisation that he barely

knew this woman struck him with the force of a hammer blow.

How could he be so attracted to a woman he barely knew?

Physical attraction was one thing, but he didn't rush into relationships no matter how strong the pull.

Particularly with vulnerable women, and if there was one thing he *did* know about Jo, it was that she was vulnerable. She had that hole in her soul she'd talked about.

Though wouldn't love fill a hole in someone's soul?

His thoughts jerked to a standstill as abruptly as a car stopping when the brakes were slammed hard.

Love?

Where had that come from?

'Cam?'

Jo's voice was tentative, no, *more* than tentative, for he heard a distinct quiver in it.

'Are we okay?' she added. 'Can we put this down as some kind of minor aberration? Can we go on as we've been going?'

He wanted to give her a hug then decided why

not? And he gathered her into his arms and hugged hard.

'Of course we're okay,' he assured her, and felt like Superman when her body lost its tension. 'But I'm not so sure about the minor aberration part. We're attracted to each other. We're both adults. Would taking that attraction further be so wrong?'

Well, yes, probably, his common sense told him, given you're not exactly cured…

'You're not staying,' she reminded him, the words muffled by his shirt as she whispered them against his chest. 'So all it could ever be is a brief affair, and…'

'And?' he prompted, although somewhere deep inside he'd have liked to suggest that he *could* stay on—that he *could* be okay again.

That he'd *like* to stay on!

But should he even be thinking about long-term commitment?

With his mind the way it was…

'And I'd be left behind with the small-town talk, the gossip, the—'

He forgot about his own reasons for not committing and concentrated on her view of things.

Got the picture immediately, even finished the sentence for her.

'Whispers and sly looks and snide smiles.'

He reached beneath her chin and tilted her head up so he could look into her eyes.

'I'm sorry, I didn't think,' he said, then he dropped a very quick kiss on her lips. Very quick because anything longer would have led not forward but back to where they'd been. 'I won't do that to you, Jo.'

Well, you brought that on yourself, Jo thought bitterly as she pushed out of the warm security of Cam's arms, eased herself across the seat—when had she, or he, undone her seat belt?—and opened the door.

'I'll walk home,' she said. 'It's only a hundred yards.'

She set off, then heard him start the rattly engine of the van, and saw the lights, dimmed, as he pulled onto the road, driving slowly enough to follow her, a careful, caring man, Fraser Cameron, just not for her.

CHAPTER TEN

AGAINST all expectations, Jo had slept soundly, waking mid-morning to a sunshine-filled day. She made herself a coffee and wandered out onto the deck, her hands cupped around the hot drink, sipping at it, waiting for the caffeine to kick in and wake her fully.

'Morning, neighbour!'

The words startled her, but it was Cam's voice that caused the sudden lurch in her stomach.

'I thought you'd be out surfing,' she grumbled, cranky at being caught in her favourite sleep attire, an ancient T-shirt of her father's worn so thin it was soft and cool and comfortable. Cranky too at the way her body had reacted to his voice, and crankiest of all that he was there, interrupting her morning commune with nature.

'Been there and done that,' he said, so bright and cheerful she wanted to hurl her cup at him—

except that it was still near-full and she needed the caffeine.

'Do you always wake up so disgustingly cheerful?' she demanded instead, slumping down into one of the low-slung canvas chairs and glaring at him across the gap between the decks.

'I've been up for hours,' he told her. 'Had a surf and a run on the beach then picked up some freshly baked pastries for breakfast. Want to share?'

He opened the paper bag he'd been holding in his hand and the scent of sweet pastries wafted across from one deck to the next. Now it was Jo's stomach talking to her, telling her how empty it was and how much it would appreciate a pastry.

Too bad! The one thing she'd decided on the short walk home the previous evening was that she should limit opportunities—outside work—for her and Cam to be together and so limit any chance of giving in to temptation as far as touching or kissing was concerned.

Though the kiss had been—spectacular!

'I'll bring them over,' he was saying, completely undaunted by the fact she hadn't answered. 'I'd say come over, but you've got better coffee. I can only do instant and I can smell yours from here.'

He's only coming for the coffee, Jo told herself, and felt a spurt of totally unnecessary disappointment, but out loud she said, very ungraciously, 'Oh, okay, come over. Let yourself in, I'll get changed.'

She hurried into her bedroom and pulled on some clothes—regular clothes, cargo pants and singlet top—pushed her fingers through her hair and clipped it up, washed her face and slathered on some moisturiser, debated lippy and told herself to get over it, then came out of the bedroom straight into the path of a frowning neighbour.

'Can I assume you've been out your front door since you got up? To get the paper, perhaps?'

Her turn to frown.

'I don't get a paper delivered,' she said, mystified by his attitude.

'Put out the cat? Let the cat in?' he persisted.

She threw up her hands in a helpless gesture.

'Have you seen a cat around here? What on earth are you on about?'

'Your front door—it was unlocked.'

He was standing so close she could feel the angry vibes he was giving off—other vibes as well, unfortunately. She stepped back but hit the wall and couldn't finish a decent retreat. Only one thing to do, stand up to him.

'So?'

His anger dissolved as quickly as it had appeared and he shook his head at her.

'Jo, I know you grew up here and to you it is still a small seaside town, little more than a big village, but times have changed. The drug culture changed not only the users but the way we all have to live. An addict in need of a fix will not hesitate to break into his own family's home to steal something to sell, and while you might not have desperate addicts here normally, right now you've got hundreds of strangers in town. You *need* to lock your doors.'

'I know, I know,' she muttered. 'I didn't need the lecture.'

She didn't add that these days she was careful about locking up, she'd just forgotten last night because she didn't want him assuming she'd forgotten because of confusion over his kiss.

Which was why she *had* forgotten, of course, she just wasn't going to admit it.

'Let's eat those pastries,' she said. 'I'll bring coffee onto the deck.'

She'd thought he'd go on out there but, no, he

followed her into the kitchen, and began opening cupboard doors, obviously in search of a plate for his offerings, but opening cupboard doors?

Wasn't that intrusive?

Jo knew it was—it was taking liberties. He was a stranger still and opening cupboard doors in her house was very intrusive.

So why did she feel a surge of pleasure—real pleasure—as if sharing her kitchen with someone was special, and comfortable, and very, very—well, nice?

She muddled her way through producing two cups of coffee, knowing now just how he liked his as she'd watched him make his own with the same machine down at the surgery.

'Tray?' he asked, and she pointed to the refrigerator, where a gap between the fridge and the wall provided a space big enough to take three bright, plastic trays.

He pulled out all three, studying them in turn, finally settling on one that had frangipani flowers all over it. He put the plate of pastries on it, two small plates, two knives—she'd missed him pulling out drawers to get the knives—then the two cups of coffee.

Jo grabbed a couple of paper napkins with

the same bright design as the tray, and dropped them on it as he lifted it from the bench. They were close, so it was inevitable their eyes should meet—meet and hold, silently communicating memories of the kiss.

Desire, hot and strong, shimmied through her body.

She turned away, not wanting him to see the signs, read the desire in her face. Determinedly thrusting the reaction aside, she led him out onto the deck, setting the small table down between two chairs in the shade as the sun was heating up.

I don't want to be doing this—

She should say it, not think it.

But saying it, she'd be lying because a lot of her was filled with pleasure over something as simple as sharing Sunday breakfast with this man.

Unfortunately the bit that wasn't filled with pleasure was shouting warnings at her, warnings only partially soothed by the pleased part telling her he was just a colleague and a neighbour and there was nothing in it.

'It's a very special place, isn't it?' he said, interrupting her internal argument.

She smiled as she agreed.

'Very special!'

She bit into a pastry and tasted the soft creamy cheese and sticky apricot in the filling, and let out a sigh of bliss.

'So is this pastry,' she told him. 'Thank you.'

Aware it sounded far too formal, especially given the heat they'd shared in the early hours of the morning, she fumbled around for some nice neutral conversation.

'Where was home for you?'

After that it was easy, Cam talked of his family, growing up in the southern suburbs of Sydney with his three sisters.

Three sisters explained a lot, Jo thought as Cam was telling her of the games they'd played as children, the camping holidays they'd had. It explained the protective attitude she'd noticed from time to time, and the instinctive rapport he seemed to have with the women at the surgery.

'And speaking of children,' he said, after he'd listed off his nieces and nephews, 'is there a particular O and G specialist you use in Port? Mrs Youngman is coming in tomorrow and I want to refer her to someone for a full examination before she goes too far with her plans for IVF.'

So the conversation slipped into work matters

and although the doctor in Jo answered quite sensibly, she hoped, the woman felt again that uneasiness in her belly. It was as if her body, against all rationality, wanted to put itself to the use for which it was designed.

Nonsense, that's all it was.

'Have you talked to Helene about the chances of conception?' she asked, to divert herself from whatever was going on inside her.

'I have,' Cam said. 'Not that I needed to. When I phoned her she knew as much as I did if not more. She'd looked up everything she could find on the internet, and although she knows the odds of conception aren't great, she's still keen.'

'I wonder why?' Jo mused, and Cam straightened in his chair.

'Does there have to be a tangible reason?' he asked. 'Couldn't it be something as simple as a strong desire to have another child? We all have two sides to us and hear two voices, one of reason and one of passion, isn't that true? And couldn't it be passion talking to her?'

Could it?

Jo answered his question with one of her own.

'Passion for someone, or passion to have a child?'

He shrugged and smiled.

'I'm a doctor, so that's not for me to know, but in general do you agree that we have the two voices?'

His eyes scanned her face and she knew he was looking for a reaction. Knew also that the conversation had shifted from Helene Youngman to something far more personal.

Something she didn't want to think about!

'I'm not sure about the passion,' she told him, shifting so she could look out to sea instead of into those probing eyes. 'Emotion certainly, but passion, I'm not so sure.'

'Of course it's passion,' he argued, touching her arm so she had to turn back and face him. 'It might be reason telling you—'

Damn it all, he's going to talk about attraction again. Her mind panicked while her body warmed, but it cooled again when he finished the sentence.

'To keep the refuge open, but it's passion that keeps you working so determinedly for it, isn't that so?'

She stared blankly at him for a moment, still lost on the path she'd thought the conversation would take.

Cam wondered what on earth had prompted him to talk of passion. He'd got a nice medical colleague-to-colleague conversation going and then blown it by bringing emotion into it—passion, in fact.

And the word had re-awoken all the physical symptoms he'd been trying to keep at bay since he'd seen Jo appear on her deck that morning, the sun shining through the fine material of her night shirt, outlining her curves in a golden glow.

He reminded himself of all the cons he'd come up with in his pros-and-cons argument when he'd got inside the flat last night—a brief affair would damage her reputation, maybe even hurt her if her feelings were engaged. And from his side, what did he have to offer? A man whose mind was cluttered with horror he was still having trouble getting over? A man who might never get back to whatever might pass for normal in this modern world?

Although wasn't that changing?

Hadn't he felt the shift?

'I suppose you could call it passion.'

The admission, spoken as if the words were being forced out against her will, caught Cam by surprise so at first he thought she was talking about their attraction—the question he'd asked forgotten as he'd followed his own twisted thoughts.

'The refuge,' she added, in a falsely patient tone, picking up on his confusion.

'Ah, yes, the refuge,' he said, but he had to smile because he suspected her thoughts had flitted to other aspects of passion, so once again they were at a crossroads of some kind.

'I'm having another cup of coffee. You?'

Was she escaping him?

He suspected she was, but now reason was back in control. It was stupid to even consider having an affair with this woman. Maybe in a year he could drift back this way. Maybe in a year he'd have come to terms with the past and be ready to look to the future—he could apply again for a position in Crystal Cove and she might even take him on…

If she hadn't married someone else in the meantime.

Now, where had that thought come from?

And why did it make his gut knot?

'Coffee,' she said again, returning to set down the two cups.

'Have you spoken to the employment agency?'

he asked, stirred up now, thinking maybe moving on wasn't such a good idea. 'About getting a woman for the job?'

She shook her head, something he loved watching her do as it always dislodged more tendrils of hair. They coiled down her neck and sprayed out from her temples.

'I haven't given it much thought. Most people who want to work over Christmas are settled into their jobs by now and won't be looking to move so I thought I'd leave it until the new year.'

He wanted to say, Keep me, but doubts tumbled in his head. He knew now he could commit to the job, but if he stayed, given the way he felt about Jo, could he commit to something else?

Like marriage?

He stood up, holding his fresh cup of coffee, and walked to the railing.

What could he offer in a marriage?

Jo had all this and he had, what?

Money in the bank for sure—overseas postings paid well—a fair amount of superannuation, a refurbished van and, yes, damn it all, still some baggage in his head.

That was what he *couldn't* offer her.

Jo had talked about the bits of self she'd lost to

love—love for her sister, her twin. His bits of self had been lost to hate—for wasn't that what war was all about?

She admitted it had taken her years to become whole again—how long would it take him?

The jangling summons of the phone somewhere inside her house broke into his thoughts, and he knew from the moment she reappeared in the doorway to the deck, white faced and anxious, that it was bad news.

'We have to go,' she said. 'An incident on the headland—Richard and Jackie Trent are up there and Richard is insisting on seeing you.'

She offered a rather fearful smile.

'So you must have got through to him the other day!'

Cam crossed the deck in three strides.

'I'm happy to go but you don't have to come, Jo,' he said. 'I know what memories the headland will throw up at you. You can wait here. Mike will keep you posted.'

'And leave Jackie and the boys without support? Leave you up there without…?'

Without what?

What could she offer Cam?

'Support,' she finished, but she knew it was a feeble imitation of what she'd like to offer him.

Which was?

Her mind was whirling.

Surely she wasn't thinking love?

Of course she was.

She was leading the way out of the house, was right inside the front door, in fact, when he stopped her with a touch on her shoulder and pulled her into his arms, hugging her tightly.

'Remember,' he whispered into her hair, 'that sometimes things just happen, without reason and without anyone being accountable. Sometimes we dig around for reasons when there aren't any.'

Cam tilted her head up so he could look into her eyes.

'You might also want to remember that I think I'm falling in love with you—maybe already fallen. Although I didn't know it until right this minute, and I admit I'm not that good a catch, that I have problems, I want you to know that I'll keep working on them. And one more thing, I am *not* moving on!'

She stared at him in disbelief but warm colour was back in her cheeks and he could feel her body straightening, her resolve stiffening, and now he knew for certain—it *was* love. For who could not love a woman who faced life with such courage— a woman about to return to the place where her sister had been so badly injured in order to help someone else?

CHAPTER ELEVEN

SURFING needed different muscles from running so the race up the path to the top of the headland had Cam puffing and panting. He only kept up with Jo because his strides were longer.

They'd parked in a cluster of police and rescue vehicles in the car park near the clubhouse. The area had been cleared of people, curious onlookers held at bay by police and volunteer rescue personnel. More police would already be on the headland, but what else would they find?

Mike came towards them as they reached the top, both of them breathing deeply to replenish the oxygen they'd used on the run.

'What's happening?' Cam asked.

'Jackie and Richard and the kids came up for a walk—Richard's suggestion—to have breakfast and go up the headland.'

Cam nodded. Jo had talked about her family doing it regularly on a Sunday morning.

'They get to the top and Richard climbs over the barrier.' Mike's voice was strained and Cam remembered he and Richard were friends.

Jo reached out and put her hand on Mike's arm.

'Someone else can tell us,' she said gently, but Mike shook his head.

'No, I'm the one who's been talking to him. He says he's no good to anyone and might as well end it now.'

Cam was thinking clearly—putting all he knew of precarious mental states to use—concentrating on Richard.

'Something happened to him,' he said to Mike. 'A year or so ago—that's when the abuse apparently started—would you know of any change in his circumstances?'

Jo was muttering to herself about the selfishness of suicides, but Cam ignored her, aware Mike was trying to think.

The policeman shook his head.

'He did have a mate—no, that couldn't be it.'

'A mate who died?' Cam guessed, but Mike shook his head.

'I know his mother died, but that was earlier. His good friend from under-nineteen cricket made the Aussie Ashes side last summer but…'

And took the place Richard might have thought was his? Cam wondered. It wasn't much to go on, but maybe it was something.

'Where are Jackie and the boys?' Jo asked, and Mike pointed to the fence, where Richard was clearly visible on the cliff-side while Jackie and the two children huddled against the safe side of the fence.

'That's your job, Jo,' Cam said. 'While I'm talking to him, see if you can ease them back, away from the fence.'

'So if something happens they won't see it?' she whispered, and he knew she was so stressed with memories and her fear for the family he wanted to hug her yet again.

He made do with a smile and hoped she'd read the hug in it.

'With me there chatting to him? Have faith, woman! I just don't want any distractions for him.'

Jo felt the smile go right through her, the heat of it melting her bones so she longed to sag against him and stay there, possibly for ever.

She stiffened her bones and her resolve and smiled back.

'Leave Jackie and the kids to me.'

Cam nodded at her, a special kind of nod that seemed to confirm a lot of things that hadn't yet been said, then he began to question Mike about Richard's request.

'Did he give any reason for wanting me?' Cam asked, as the two men moved towards the fence, Jo following but not too close. She could hear the waves crashing on the rocks, feel the thud of their power beneath her feet, but her fear now wasn't from her memories, but for Cam.

'No, just said he wants to talk to you—asked for you in particular,' Mike was saying as the two men reached the high point of the headland where a safety fence, eight feet high, had been erected.

Jackie and the two boys were crouched in a pathetic heap, crying helplessly.

'Wait until I'm talking to him then ease them slowly away because if he does jump they don't want that memory in their heads for ever,' Cam said quietly to Jo, although he knew the advice was unnecessary. If anyone would know what best to do for the little family, it was Jo, whose mantle of care was like a blanket spread across the whole Cove.

But right now he had to stop thinking about her—stop thinking about anyone but the man who was in such agony of spirits that death seemed the only option.

'Do you want me this side or that, Richard?' he asked.

He spoke quietly but he knew from the gasp behind him that Jo had heard the question—knew too how fearful she must be to see someone else's life in danger on the headland.

'You'd come over?' Richard was asking.

'Of course,' Cam said. 'I might not be able to climb it as easily as you—I'm not built for climbing—but I think I could make it.'

Richard seemed to consider this for a moment.

'Why would you want to?'

'I thought maybe if I was closer to you I could see what you're seeing more clearly,' Cam told him. 'It's hard to know what people are thinking, but we should be able to see what they're seeing and right now I'd like to know what you're seeing that makes you think life's not worth living.'

'Well, you can see that easy enough,' Richard said. 'I'm no good, that's why!'

'No one's no good,' Cam said.

'I'm no good,' Richard repeated, although the words lacked the conviction the first assertion had.

'Of course you are. We all think that about ourselves from time to time. Look at me—a trained doctor and psychologist yet I'm surfing my way along the coast, looking for a purpose in life. I believed I'd failed the young soldiers I was supposed to help and I let myself forget the good I could do, the help I could give people. I bet you've forgotten the things about you that made Jackie fall in love with you—make her still love you as I'm sure she does.'

'That's different,' Richard muttered, but Cam saw he'd moved a little bit away from the edge.

'Not so very different. I had to learn to live with the guilt and feelings of helplessness. They might never go away but I'm learning to handle them now—learning to accept them, not run away from them. *You* have to learn to live with your temper, how to control it or how to walk away when you can't control it. From the little I know of you, you're not stupid. You can learn to handle the problem, and once you've told your friends about it, they'll help you every step along the way. My problem was I never talked about the horrors that I saw. I tried not to even think about them. Stuff you bottle in just festers but, like an infected wound, once you open it up, it will heal.'

Cam knew he was following good psychological

processes using personal admissions so Richard didn't feel he was the only one with a problem, but was it working?

Would Richard think it all a con?

Of all the people gathered on the headland, Jo was the only one who'd know he, Cam, was speaking from his heart. Would she know also that it was because of her he'd changed? Because of her he'd moved on?

He hoped so, just as he hoped he could talk Richard off this cliff, but reason told him he couldn't get through to Richard while they were on opposite sides of an eight foot fence. He sighed inwardly and put a foot into the wire mesh.

'I'm coming over,' he said. 'It's best we sit together if we're going to talk.'

No reply but once again Richard inched further from the edge, giving Cam a spurt of hope. Somehow he clambered over the fence, ungainly as a hippo scaling a wall, then he settled beside Richard on the grassy ledge, trying hard to ignore the waves crashing on the rocks beneath them. Heights had never been his favourite places.

Richard started talking, unprompted, asking him questions about the army, asking him how men who'd seen horrors in their lives could learn to live with them, and it occurred to Cam that Richard's mate getting into the Aussie cricket team was probably not a trigger for his violence but a final straw.

'I went into the army because my family had always had army people in it—my dad and grandfather and a long string before them. What about you? I don't even know what work you do,' Cam said, thinking perhaps something in Richard's job might lie at the root of his problems.

'I'm an accountant but I do volunteer work for the SES.'

Ha! The flat tones as he'd spoken told Cam more than the words themselves, although the SES? The State Emergency Service was made up of volunteers—the members called out to all manner of emergencies, from floods to fires, to searches for missing children, and multi-car pile-ups on the highway.

'That's got its fair share of horror,' Cam said quietly, and Richard nodded, then he began to cry.

'She was only four, younger than Aaron, and I was the one who found her. I should have been happy—well, not happy but relieved her parents had got some kind of closure. But all I felt was anger—anger at a useless waste of life—anger aimed not only at the man who'd abducted her but at myself and all human beings that we allow such things to happen. I didn't know the anger was building inside me. I thought I was okay—I mean, it was six months later. Then the doctor said Jackie—said we—said the baby would be a girl, and something just cracked inside me...'

Cam put his arms around Richard's shoulders and held him while he bled out his pain in stumbling words and shattered sentences, the little girl, his boys, helplessness and anger.

'I knew I must have killed Jackie's love when that happened, and that made me angrier because she kept saying it didn't matter and she loved me and I kept thinking it *had* to be a lie.'

Cam held him tightly, knowing that further along the fence, where it ended near the northern edge of the cliff, the emergency crew was quietly cutting through the wire mesh. He hoped that was all they were doing. Prayed they didn't have some mad rescue plan to suddenly rush at him and Richard with the two of them sitting so close to almost certain death.

Back behind the main stage of the drama, Jo

stayed with Jackie, the two boys having been taken back down the path by Jackie's parents.

Every atom in Jo's body wanted to move forward, to force her hand through the mesh and get a grip on Cam's clothing.

As if that would keep him safe!

She sighed, shaking her head in disbelief at the pain she was feeling—the pain that fear was pumping through her body—fear for a man she'd known only a week.

Could people fall in love in a week?

Cam had said he loved her—or had he said falling in love—either way, love was part of the equation, but could it be real, could it be possible, could it last, something that happened so quickly?

She should have told him how *she* was feeling.

How *was* she feeling?

Afraid! That's what.

And muddled.

And probably in love...

Cam eased himself away from Richard, needing to look into his face as he spoke to him.

'There's so much help available,' he said quietly. 'For a start, there are ways of helping you come to terms with the terrible things you experienced when you found the little girl. And once you can learn to live with those memories, you'll find a lot of the anger has gone and even if it hasn't, you can learn what triggers it, and what other ways you might be able to do to handle those triggers. Right now, you have a wonderful opportunity to begin to change. I'm not saying it will be easy, but isn't it worth giving it a go? You obviously love your family very dearly. Wouldn't it be worth getting help so you can keep on loving them—and they can keep on loving you?'

'They're better off without me!'

Cam felt his gut knot. For the first time Richard had stated his intention, which, given the place, was obviously to jump.

Did that mean he, Cam, was losing the argument?

That he wasn't getting through to him?

He had to try again—try harder.

'Are they?' Cam asked, reaching out to rest his hand on Richard's forearm. 'Look at me, Richard, and tell me honestly, will your boys be better off growing up without a father, without your love—without even knowing how much you love them? Jumping off is the easy way out. You don't have to put any effort into that—believe me, I know it—

but is it any way to show you love those boys—to show Jackie that you love her? She loves you very much or she wouldn't have gone back to you, but is leaving her to battle on on her own any way to repay that love? Of course it isn't. You have to fight for love. In your case, you have to fight the things inside you that are hurting the love you have for her. You can do that—you can conquer those ghosts—and your future with your family will be so much stronger and better and brighter because you *have* conquered them.'

Cam saw Richard's eyes widen, almost as if they needed to be bigger, to take in all he was saying. Cam held his gaze, hoping to force his message into Richard's brain while his own brain was questioning the words he'd said, the bits about fighting for love, turning them around to examine them more closely, picking out the bits that could apply to him—to him and Jo.

Conquering ghosts and going on stronger— those bits particularly.

Cam hauled his mind back to the man with him on the ledge.

'Richard?'

'I can't go back now,' he said, and moved his legs.

Despair reverberated through Cam's body, and despair ignited anger, but he held it in check.

'Because you think going back would be cowardly? Because you think if you turn around now and walk away people will think you weren't brave enough to jump?'

Richard turned away from him, but Cam grabbed his shoulder and gave him a little shake.

'Believe me,' he said, 'walking away now will probably be the bravest thing you've ever done because it will mean you've faced up to things that are wrong and you're willing to put them right. Walking away is like a warrior putting on his suit of armour and preparing for war, because what lies ahead is going to be far harder than jumping off a cliff. Except for Jackie, every person behind the fence at the moment is a trained professional and they will understand that by walking back you're making the courageous choice. Then there's Jackie and you know damn well that if you don't walk back through there you'll break her heart.'

Finally Richard nodded. Cam helped the emotionally exhausted man to his feet and Jackie's desperate cry of 'Richard' echoed over their heads. Richard turned and looked towards the cry and Jackie escaped Jo's hold and raced to the fence, taking Richard's hand through the mesh. Like that, holding and releasing fingers through the diamond shaped wires they walked to the cut in the fence, where Jackie fell into his arms.

CHAPTER TWELVE

IT WAS mesmerising, seeing love like that, Jackie and Richard, their fingers looping then parting, all the way along the mesh.

So mesmerising, in fact, that it wasn't until they'd reached the gap that Jo realised Cam wasn't following along behind.

Her heart stopped beating until she traced her way back along the mesh and saw him, sitting down again, leaning back against the fence, still only inches from the edge of the cliff, totally drained of all energy by the tension of the situation.

She sprinted towards the gap, eased past the policeman who was guarding it, and walked carefully along the narrow lip beyond the fence. Reaching Cam, she sat down beside him, resolutely banishing memories of Jilly from her mind.

She tucked her hand into his, and just held on

for a while, then, as she felt his tension easing, she spoke.

'Walk you back?'

She said it quietly, not urging him in any way, knowing, for all the hurtful memories the place held, she'd be content to sit—for ever if necessary—until he was ready to leave.

She looked out at the ocean, reasonably calm today, so the waves sloshed rather than crashed against the cliff. The mighty power was leashed, but for how long?

She thought of Jilly, and, looking out at the mighty Pacific, she said goodbye. Oh, her sister, her twin, would live on in her heart, but Cam's arrival in the Cove had shifted Jo's perspective.

Cam's arrival?

Or love's arrival?

Still uncertain, she only knew that things had changed.

'We have to go forward,' she said quietly, 'moving into the sunshine, and letting the shadows fall behind us.'

Cam turned and put his arm around her shoulders, drawing her close.

'That's a thought to hold on to, isn't it?' he said softly, pressing a kiss against her temple.

'Can Richard do it? Will he be all right?' Jo asked.

'I don't know,' Cam answered honestly. 'We can only hope and be there for him and try in every way we can to help him.'

'You're a good man, Fraser Cameron,' Jo said quietly, but her voice was distracted and he could only guess at the thoughts that must be racing through her head. Her mention of going forward had told him so much. Sitting here was helping her not just to say goodbye to her sister but maybe let go of a little of the guilt and grief she'd carried in her heart for far too long.

She snuggled closer and he held her, wanting to prolong this special time together.

Special time?

Why would he think that?

'We should move,' she said, but she didn't make a start and with her warm and shapely body tucked against his, he didn't feel like arguing.

Mike put a stop to this indulgence.

'If you two stay much longer you'll have to climb back over, and I can charge you for being there, you know.'

Jo muttered to herself. Bloody Mike! Just when she was getting herself back together, not to mention revelling being in Cam's arms, so tightly held, so safe and warm, Mike had to go and spoil it.

She waited for Cam to tell Mike they were coming, but he remained silent and she realised, with a rush overwhelming delight, that he was leaving the decision up to her. That he had no intention of moving until she was ready.

Which led to a further revelation that what Cam had said about loving her must be more than words for only someone who really loved her would consider staying here with her and eventually having to climb the fence.

Again!

'We'd better go,' she murmured.

'Okay,' he said, and with that he put his arms around and lifted her to her feet.

'A truly gallant knight would carry you all the way but for all your slight build you're no light-weight and if I staggered and missed my footing we'd both go crashing to the rocks beneath, then Richard would have more guilt to deal with and he'd come and jump and—'

'Okay, I get the picture,' Jo told him, laughing up at him, reading the concern behind the non-sense he was spouting. 'We'll walk together.'

And they did, one step in front of the other,

holding the fence with one hand, their other hands linked between them.

'It was a metaphor for life, that walk,' Cam said later, when, all official business done, they sat on the deck, their chairs close but not touching, eating pizza and looking out to sea. 'Taking one step at a time, that's all we can do. Looking to the sun, as you said earlier.'

He put down his crust and turned towards her.

'Could you possibly see your way clear to take those steps with me?' he asked, his blue eyes watching her intently, the tension in his face betraying the worry behind his almost casual words.

Jo was as a loss. She knew for sure she wanted to go forward in her life with this man—to take those steps beside him—but so much remained unspoken—love had come too fast.

'Might it not be love?'

As soon as the words were out there, she realised they'd not spoken of love—not really—so maybe he wasn't offering it.

Although earlier he'd said—

But *she* hadn't.

Now Cam was smiling at her and her heart was melting so maybe it *was* love.

'I can't speak for you,' he said, lifting her hand

and raising it to his lips, pressing kisses on her fingers, one by one, then turning her hand to kiss her palm, a sensation that sent tingles up her spine. 'But for me it's love and, yes, we can say it's come too soon, how can we know, and all of that, but my voice of reason tells me it can't be anything else, while my voice of passion—well, it's best we wait until we're in a dimly lit room without our clothes on before I let it talk.'

He paused, tucking her hand tightly into his and holding it.

'I'm not a great catch, I realise that—the baggage, for one thing—but I can promise you my love for ever, Jo, for what it's worth, and should you love me back, I'll treasure your love above all else.'

'Even surfing?' Jo teased, because his words were causing chaos in her body and confusion in her mind and she needed to break the tension sparking in the air around them.

He tightened his hand momentarily on hers, then smiled as he released it, giving it one last kiss before returning it to her lap.

'Now you're pushing it,' he growled, but his eyes were repeating the messages his lips had given earlier and Jo knew she had to answer.

No more jokes.

She clambered out of her deck chair and moved so she could kneel in front of him, her hands on his knees, looking up into his face.

'What woman could not love a man who makes smiley-face fruit breakfasts for her, who listens to her dredge up all her guilt and anguish, who understands that sometimes there's no need for words, especially when a hug is available?'

'But?' he prompted, no doubt guessing that her cautious self—*her* voice of reason—would be yelling at her.

'What do you think?' It was like a dare—a challenge—to see if he knew her as well as he seemed to think he did.

'You're thinking it's too soon—love can't happen in a week—but, Jo, darling, something has happened, so let's follow the path it's set us on and see where it leads. The steps I want to take with you can be baby steps, not great huge strides. For now, it's enough for me to know you're on the journey with me.'

The pause was probably infinitesimal yet it seemed to Jo to stretch for ever.

Then, 'Well,' he added, and she stood up, hauling on his hands so he, too, had to stand. She moved into his welcoming arms, pressed herself against his chest and whispered her answer.

A simple 'Yes', no qualifications, no doubts or hesitation, just 'Yes' to let him know she wanted to walk into the future with him, whether with baby steps or huge strides—they would be doing it together.

She wore the ring he gave her for the first time at the raising of the Christmas tree. Crystal Cove had a sister city—although neither town could qualify for city—in Norway, which sent a Christmas tree every year.

The raising of the tree was the biggest public event of the year in the small town, so Jo was aware her action wouldn't go unnoticed.

But two weeks after Cam's proposal she was so in love that not wearing it wasn't an option. Not only did she want everyone to know she was engaged, she wanted everyone to realise just how much she loved the man who'd come, more or less by accident, into her life.

'So, they raise the tree?' They were driving down to the esplanade where the tree would reign supreme until the new year when Cam asked the question. 'Pull it up with ropes while we all watch?'

Jo grinned at him.

'It's more than that! You'll see. In fact, as we're in the official party thanks to Helene Youngman thinking you're the bee's knees, you'll get an excellent view.'

To Cam's surprise the tree wasn't just a tree. Well, it *was*—a huge, weighty pine—but its boughs were already hung with decorations and once it was in place in a specially designed container, someone would flick a switch and it would rise up into position, brilliant in its splendour, a focal point of the Cove's Christmas.

Even with the tree still resting on the ground, Jo's face shone with happiness, and he marvelled that with all the pain she'd had in her life, the open, innocent delight of a child was still there inside her—inside this woman he loved.

And looking at the tree, all ready to be raised, and at the faces of the people all around it, waiting for the yearly ceremony, he realised that the same joy in simple pleasures was inside him as well. Apart from surfing, he'd thought he'd lost all that, but obviously finding love—finding Jo—had given it back to him.

He turned to her and put his arms around her, bending to kiss her on her lips.

'What's that for?' she demanded, being Jo, and he smiled at her.

'For giving me back the power to look at a Christmas tree and smile—to see enjoyment and know I'm sharing it—to feel what other people are feeling—simple pleasure.'

Now she kissed him, standing up on tiptoe.

'*Has* to be love, doesn't it?' she whispered.

'It *has* to be,' he confirmed.

* * * * *

July

THE BOSS SHE CAN'T RESIST	Lucy Clark
HEART SURGEON, HERO...HUSBAND?	Susan Carlisle
DR LANGLEY: PROTECTOR OR PLAYBOY?	Joanna Neil
DAREDEVIL AND DR KATE	Leah Martyn
SPRING PROPOSAL IN SWALLOWBROOK	Abigail Gordon
DOCTOR'S GUIDE TO DATING IN THE JUNGLE	Tina Beckett

August

SYDNEY HARBOUR HOSPITAL: LILY'S SCANDAL	Marion Lennox
SYDNEY HARBOUR HOSPITAL: ZOE'S BABY	Alison Roberts
GINA'S LITTLE SECRET	Jennifer Taylor
TAMING THE LONE DOC'S HEART	Lucy Clark
THE RUNAWAY NURSE	Dianne Drake
THE BABY WHO SAVED DR CYNICAL	Connie Cox

September

FALLING FOR THE SHEIKH SHE SHOULDN'T	Fiona McArthur
DR CINDERELLA'S MIDNIGHT FLING	Kate Hardy
BROUGHT TOGETHER BY BABY	Margaret McDonagh
ONE MONTH TO BECOME A MUM	Louisa George
SYDNEY HARBOUR HOSPITAL: LUCA'S BAD GIRL	Amy Andrews
THE FIREBRAND WHO UNLOCKED HIS HEART	Anne Fraser

October

GEORGIE'S BIG GREEK WEDDING?	Emily Forbes
THE NURSE'S NOT-SO-SECRET SCANDAL	Wendy S. Marcus
DR RIGHT ALL ALONG	Joanna Neil
SUMMER WITH A FRENCH SURGEON	Margaret Barker
SYDNEY HARBOUR HOSPITAL: TOM'S REDEMPTION	Fiona Lowe
DOCTOR ON HER DOORSTEP	Annie Claydon

November

SYDNEY HARBOUR HOSPITAL: LEXI'S SECRET	Melanie Milburne
WEST WING TO MATERNITY WING!	Scarlet Wilson
DIAMOND RING FOR THE ICE QUEEN	Lucy Clark
NO.1 DAD IN TEXAS	Dianne Drake
THE DANGERS OF DATING YOUR BOSS	Sue MacKay
THE DOCTOR, HIS DAUGHTER AND ME	Leonie Knight

December

SYDNEY HARBOUR HOSPITAL: BELLA'S WISHLIST	Emily Forbes
DOCTOR'S MILE-HIGH FLING	Tina Beckett
HERS FOR ONE NIGHT ONLY?	Carol Marinelli
UNLOCKING THE SURGEON'S HEART	Jessica Matthews
MARRIAGE MIRACLE IN SWALLOWBROOK	Abigail Gordon
CELEBRITY IN BRAXTON FALLS	Judy Campbell